ALSO BY REBECCA LAWTON

Reading Water: Lessons from the River
Junction, Utah
Write Free: Attracting the Creative Life
Discover Nature in the Rocks: Things to Know and Things to Do
Sacrament: Homage to a River

Steelies and Other Endangered Species

Stories on Water

Rebecca Lawton

A LITTLE CURLEW PRESS
TRADE PAPERBACK

Steelies and Other Endangered Species: Stories on Water
Copyright © 2014 by Rebecca Lawton

ISBN: #978-0-9960825-0-1
Library of Congress Control Number: 2014940987

Cover Design: James Knake

Cover Photo: Gary O'Boyle

CREDITS

Earlier versions of these stories were published in the following journals and anthologies. "An Exposition of the Development of the Earth," *Slippage*, Volume 2, February 2014; "Marooned" as "Change of Heart," *The Acorn: A Journal of the Western Sierra*, El Dorado, California, El Dorado Writers' Guild, 1995; "The Road to Bonanza," *Midway Journal*, June 2011; "The Middle of a River in Flood," *Standing Wave*, Prescott, Arizona, 1997; "Sandstone," THEMA, Metairie, Louisiana, *THEMA* Literary Society, 1995; "Sipapu," *Milk & Ink: A Mosaic of Motherhood*, Denver, Outskirts Press, 2010; "Steelies," *Connotations*, Sitka, Alaska, The Island Institute, 2011; "Weaker than Water," performed as "Only Water" by Page on Stage, Santa Rosa and Rohnert Park, CA, Glaser Center and KRCB Radio 91.1 FM, 2006; "What I Never Told You," *Walking the Twilight*, Flagstaff, Arizona, Northland Publishing, 1994; "The Wish," *Perigree: Publication for the Arts*, Volume 7, Issue 3, April 2010.

For my grandparents

Austin and Marjorie Frost,
R.E. Lawton, Sr., and Jenny Lawton

who taught me the value of nature
and importance of art.

Nothing is weaker than water. Yet for overcoming what is hard and strong, nothing surpasses it. — Lao-Tzu

CONTENTS

Author's note: Although these stories are fictional, the wild rivers and lives in them are not.

Steelies
and
Other Endangered Species:
Stories on Water

What I Never Told You

You came to the Canyon after the war and left when you had to—years later, when the sons of bitches we worked for let you go. Everybody besides them knew the river was the best place for you, with its sidecanyons and grottoes, maybe the only place a guy could stand to live after two years of hell in a strange jungle. Other vets were going crazy when they came home, never fitting in, sometimes taking a brother or lover with them when they went off. Because what's a man supposed to do, get a desk job? After he's been trained to slit the throats of his sleeping enemies? After he's walked point in utter darkness, developed a sixth sense for trip wires? Even now, though I'm thinking you might have left the river sooner, I can't picture you ever working in some darkened office, eating microwaved meals and staring at a windowless wall. On the river you found your perfect niche.

Damn you anyway. When the cops called that day, I slammed down the phone mid-sentence. I told the one cop he lied, that he didn't know you. Maybe I screamed at him—I don't

1

know—for being wrong about you. He didn't get that you were just out of place. Back on the river there was room for you. You could live under the sky, use your knife every day, feel a rush in the biggest rapids. You could work with ropes, coil them, tie them, pull and cut them. You'd wear your boots, those green-and-black hightops you never took off. Even at night you wore them, your feet sticking toes down into the sand past the end of your groundcloth.

Nights when you fell asleep halfway down the beach or up in the kitchen, wherever you finished a bottle, I'd cover you with your blanket. But I wouldn't touch the boots. You said wearing them around the clock pulled you through more than one night raid—nasty skirmishes other foot soldiers never survived.

You'd been on the river ten years before I came there, young, ready for everything. You were the veteran boatman; I was the eager trainee. You swept like one more drop of water into the foam and waves and sharp falls that together pounded loud and thunderous. You'd spent nights under the dark sky and bright stars, watching the glow on far rims after the moon goes down. You had the distance in you.

I drew to you as fast as water runs off stone. Who could've resisted? I'd come to the Canyon to learn the rapids, the names of sidecanyons, the best route through Lava Falls, how to survive the heat. You knew it all. You could show me. Since coming home you'd spent every summer rowing long days against the wind, setting up camps after dark and lining up for the bubble line entry at Lava. You'd probably run all the rapids a hundred times, mostly nerve ending and a mumbled prayer, the same way you say you walked point. You may have lost your soul to the war, your youth to an Asian whore, but your heart still beat hot and fast.

At the oars you showed an artist's skill and a madman's flair, detached from fear in a God-given way. To you, the hairball entry at Crystal Rapids was the world's greatest cakewalk, a waltz with another great giant. I could only watch in awe alongside the other members of the crew. But being the only female, my unspoken wonder worked two ways: I knew that your hair curled at the nape of your neck, that you stood tan and tall, all parts intact. I knew about the difference in your eyes, their haunted and startled look. They drew me. I fought a growing urge to touch you—but what to do with a man who tells terrifying war stories? When you caught me looking, you blinked, then smiled so dazzlingly wide the hope of every angel crashed in on my heart.

Of all places, we kissed first at the Flagstaff drive-in. Ironic, after what the police said when they called, but true. We'd been together on a real river, leading people through glades of single-leafed ash and cottonwood near clear-running pools. But we never kissed until we huddled on one of those asphalt bumps built up for cars to face the big movie screen.

We'd driven out under a striped sky, crimson at the dark earth and lavender up higher, then indigo under the first spread of stars. Just off the trip and smelling shower-clean, you looked handsome in a pair of new jeans and light summer shirt. I wore a blouse and long skirt. You kept your big hand on my knee, moving only to shift gears. We parked outside the chain-link fence and hoisted up a blanket before we climbed over to the right side of the lot, where only a few cars had parked. We spread the blanket for us and a window speaker as nighthawks dipped near lightpoles. Sagebrush and popcorn scent carried on the evening breeze. You left to fetch snacks as the title, *The Corpse Grinders*, blasted onto the screen. Your laugh reached back from the refreshment stand. When you returned, I pulled you to me. We giggled and huddled together as the corpse grinders fed chopped human liver to rampant killer cats.

Soon you lay on and around me, rolling in my arms on the blanket and asphalt, your breath smelling thick of smoke and beer. I kept my mouth open to kiss you. Your hands snaked under my blouse and skirt, your callouses felt rough on my clean skin, breasts, and belly.

"Oh la la," you whispered. I rubbed your boots with my toes, groped for your jeans, tugged open your fly. Inside were coarse, curled hairs and smooth skin. I dug deeper, then pulled my hand away too fast when I felt you, knowing I shouldn't. I tried to reach in again, but you rolled away.

"I can't." You cried.

I'd guessed that. You'd felt limp as string. I brushed tiny rocks from your hair as I cursed the hard ground of the Flagstaff drive-in. Maybe it would have gone better on some beach on the river, in the sand still warm from the summer sun. You sobbed as I covered you in the thin camp blanket—it was yours, government issue.

"Forget it, R.J." You shook your head. You could never have anything normal with me. If you loved me, I'd leave you, too.

I got that. You'd already told me about John from Twin Falls, who'd wanted to come home to raise quarter horses. And Henry from Helena, who'd planned to manage his dad's hunting lodge. You'd outlived your whole squad, all nine men blown away like leaves, not once but twice. The second time you'd made it by burrowing under the dead bodies of your buddies until the V.C. swept through. If I'd pried more, I would have shared your nightmare: crushed intestines, fixed stares, pumping blood. Better men than you, you claimed—and here you were.

The credits rolled as car engines started across the drive-in. We climbed back over the fence to walk to your vehicle, the Chevy El Camino with a rack built of beat-up, sawn-off oars. We rode back to town, toward crystalline streetlights in a clear

August night. You drove me back to the boathouse, though I'd said I'd go with you to Williams, to anywhere. Maybe we could just drive all night and figure things out. But you dropped me off fast. No wonder your words stunned me. You were in love with me, you said. You pulled the truck door closed. Your taillights moved away under the other red lights in town, the blink-blinking aircraft-warning signals up on the peaks.

But try telling all that to the police. Ask anybody, not just the cops I talked to, to take a heart as big as the world and give it some shit. Rough it up really good, then turn it loose and see how it does. Or just watch a star fall, or a bird blow to earth in a storm.

Our little window slammed shut as fast as it had opened, just as the summer season was ending. September pressed in. The crew had told me you drank more toward the end of the season—really, everybody did as dread crept in about winter jobs and colder weather. But you gave it your full devotion, and I knew better than to break up that love affair. The nights I had to cover you grew more frequent. Soon you were falling asleep out of your bag every night, curled up on the beach near a bottle. You were getting harder to wake each morning. The crew sent me to do it, thinking a woman's voice would upset you the least, not thinking what it might mean to me to see you huddled alone on the sand.

Flocks of egrets moved upstream, on to somewhere, as fall pushed them upriver. The pairs of ducks we saw didn't linger in pools; no more stopping and starting and letting us chase them downstream late afternoons. They flew right through the Canyon, and I watched you watch the birds move on.

No doubt about it: drink didn't improve your disposition. In that you were no exception. The crew knew to give you room the morning after, but the passengers didn't. And you had to go and mix a hangover with our scheduled day at Havasu Creek. Talk about your worst combination. Havasu was the spookiest place on the river for you, the most reminiscent of the jungle, the only sidecanyon so tangled with wild grape and overgrown cottonwood and willow it put you right back in the war. I'd seen you beside Havasu Creek in a full sweat, first thing in the morning, just remembering. I'd seen you talking to yourself, your face covered with tears, your features twisted. It was the only place I witnessed your dialogue with demons, usually hidden or silent. Maybe if the New York lawyer's wife had snuck up behind you on a good morning at another creek, you'd have kept your job.

I didn't see what happened, but I heard it: twin screams, yours and hers. Later she confessed between sobs that she had run up tippy-toe behind you to tap on your shoulder—you who could hear footsteps or a whisper fifty yards away. But you were lost in the jungle that day. You'd whirled on her—tall in your instant ferocity—spun her and held your knife to her throat. As soon as you did it, you realized your mistake, as soon as the knife pressed to soft flesh. Of the screams I heard, I remember yours, anguished and terrible.

You let her go. She squealed and ran for the boats.

By the time I saw you through the wild grape, your fate had been sealed. First I noticed your boots on the trail, then I saw a man wearing them who wasn't recognizable. You looked crumpled, your sun shirt torn and half-tucked into your cutoffs. You turned to the creek and threw away your knife. It struck a midstream boulder, clattered, and fell into the turquoise water. I opened my mouth to call your name, and you whirled in the path. You stared and swayed, a world away.

I tried but couldn't call your name. My mouth opened and closed, opened and closed, no sound coming out.

You squinted. I waved. Unsmiling, you peered, turned, and lurched into a trailside ocotillo. You weaved and staggered down the path, hobbling out of sight, headed for the boats and the river.

In early December of that year, you started calling me. You didn't reveal much over the telephone, just laughed and said you were fine. You were sure you'd be back on the river next season. Some veteran's program was working wonders, but I never found out where it was. Each time, I asked for your number. Each time, you didn't tell me. Instead you teased, drawing out my name—*Arrr Jay, Arrr Jay*—then hung up the phone. Once when your voice was clear and strong, you said, "Just remember one thing, R.J.—I'm in love with you," then signed off. I wanted to whisper sweet words back, but you were gone too soon, and the line went dead. When you called around Christmas, your voice was slurred. After that, I heard only from the police, who said my number had been in your wallet.

Now I know you'd been living in your truck, maybe even since September. The last place you'd had a meal and a shower under one roof may have been back at the boathouse in Flagstaff. And it wasn't even the cops who found you. Two guys on a cleanup crew saw you in your locked car after showtime at a drive-in in Bakersfield. They pounded on your window. They shouted at you to "wake up, mister, the movie's been over for an hour." When they couldn't rouse you, they called the police.

The cop read me the coroner's report: adult male, veteran of the Vietnam War. Williams, Arizona, address. Thirty-six years old. Alcoholic seizure. Found in street clothes and combat boots.

The cop said, too, that the coroner was amazed you could wear any kind of shoe. "Pair of wicked bone spurs. Never could have passed selective service."

I told him your feet must've been normal—you'd been drafted. You'd not only been called up, you'd served. It was the war that drove you crazy; no way you'd been born like that. I told him the truth and slammed down the receiver. Soon as I did, I picked it up again. There was a lot I could tell them. They didn't know you slept with your boots on, face down mostly, that you worked on the river and could sleep anywhere, even in the cab of your truck. You'd gone cold turkey and were going to work again next season. You had things to look forward to. You were in love with me.

It wasn't a cop's voice I heard then—just dial tone. No words. Just a whine lonelier than silence, lonelier even than a river's hush when winter's coming. Nothing from me, either. Just my mouth opening and closing, opening and closing, no sound coming out.

Sipapu

True hugged her husband goodbye as the storm blew in. She stared over his shoulder at a flock of blackbirds that settled on soil she'd turned for a garden. "Don't worry about me, True," Doug said, stepping into his pickup. "I'll just be nose to grindstone." With her artist's eye for detail, True observed the first flakes of snow falling as big and soft as rose petals, at first not sticking but instead melting away from the dark, brown soil. Gray and low, the sky's overcast moved fast, with shrinking views of cobalt blue between the clouds. As Doug started his ignition, the blackbirds scared up to a tree True hated, a fruitless mulberry on the property line.

The forecast had promised a late-season blizzard, and within hours a heavy snowfall closed the mountain road behind Doug. True paced the house. She knew he wouldn't call her until the road reopened. His cell phone barely got reception up at the ski shed, and his company had an emergency-only landline policy during snow-ins. Usually she agreed that not talking during work hours was wise, but this was different. He knew her test results from Dr. Martin. She'd shared them as soon as she'd learned them.

True moved ghost like from window to window, looking out. She could have played the radio or watched the news but didn't. Twin Peaks, where Doug worked, was obscured by clouds. The plot of soil that had attracted the blackbirds lay under a foot of powder and still the snow came. Snowplows growled through the neighborhood but couldn't keep the roads clear.

Illness stirred her gut. Waves of nausea had begun after their last lovemaking and stayed insistent. Why did they call it morning sickness? It was all-the-time sickness—bile on her tongue, inertia in every limb. She felt worst when she hadn't eaten, so she devoured salt-water crackers. She couldn't paint because the strong smell of the oils repelled her. If she opened the tubes or spent time in their presence, she'd give up food altogether. She turned her thoughts to escaping with Doug for their planned week away. If they were still going, she mused.

She dialed him, phone policy or no, putting the call through the central operator. A machine voice answered at the Helicopter Shed. "Hello! You've reached Snow Eagle Adventures. We're out skiing the steep and deep! Please leave a message—" True hung up.

She pulled on pack boots. At least she could dig out the driveway and clear off her old Volvo wagon. She bundled up and stepped out the back door, where the chill brought immediate tears. She fought against the roiling in her stomach as she scraped the ground with the wide shovel blade. Below the snow's titanium-oxide white, asphalt showed the color of graphite—it would make a good study in contrasts. She finished and went inside to rest.

Doug returned home near dark on the third day, when she was clearing the driveway for the fifth or so time. He drove in without a pause and met her as she replaced the shovel on the back steps. Snowflakes turned to water droplets on his sepia hair and Prussian blue fleece. His eyes looked opaque and rimmed with the raccoon rings he got when he hadn't slept. "Thank God you're here," he said. "I forgot my key."

"Of course I'm here. We're supposed to start our vacation week." She heard the edge in her own voice.

He sighed. "Let's go in."

Indoors, the stuffy air overwhelmed her. She entered as far as the living room while he made two stops: the bathroom for a voluminous pee and the bedroom to collapse on their queen bed. Within minutes the sound of his snoring drifted back to where she listened from the old loveseat. His rattled breathing, usually so endearing, annoyed her. His snoring shifted to a low *putt-putt-putt*. She felt bile rise in her throat again. He'd said nothing about their trip. Nothing about how she was feeling.

They'd spoken about it just once, in bed together the night before the storm. At first their closeness in the sheets felt warm and easy. He skimmed her body with a touch as breezy as silken wings, a mere brush that seemed near and far away at the same time.

She said, "Talk to me. Say what you're thinking."

He kissed her right eyelid. It stuck shut a few seconds. "You're beautiful. I love your burnt umber hair and chromium-green eyes." He'd matched them to her oils one day while she composed a still life with coffee and apples.

"But do you want to keep it this time?"

He sighed and rolled away. "Aw, True, I'm still just a kid myself."

She felt her heart fall. To return to the special clinic, to be sucked clean—she didn't think she could face it again. Tears would run into her ears as she stared at the ceiling and felt a new hollow space inside her. The last time, she'd felt the small life pass out of her while the stranger doctor frowned just inches from her face. He'd asked, "How will you be more careful in the future?"

She'd promised him they'd use a condom as well as her daily pill. But Doug had refused.

"That's what the damn pills are for," he'd said.

She had done her weeping in private. Luckily her river-guide sister, R.J., had been off work that week and could keep True company by phone. R.J. had sent roses, Mars violet heirlooms. "Where's Doug?" she'd asked.

"On the mountain. Leading a group of heli-skiers from Texas."

True slept well the night Doug returned but startled awake when she noticed he'd gone again. The blanket on his side of the bed was turned down, the steel gray sheets rumpled. Another shift after three straight nights on the mountain? Unheard of. A note on the kitchen table read, "Called back to work—2 a.m.— road closing again." The driveway showed the pressed-down tracks of his departure, dotted with fresh pellets of rind snow. The back porch still bore footprints from his driving boots.

True cleared powder from both sets of steps, then returned to the kitchen where a blinking light on the phone machine signaled a call had come in. She punched the button, eager to hear. It was R.J., calling from the Flagstaff bungalow she rented with another Grand Canyon guide. "Hey, True, are you and Doug still coming down? The futon awaits. Call me!"

Packing didn't take long. On the blank backside of Doug's note, True wrote her own. Short and to the point, she thought. Calling her sister back, she left a message saying she was on her way. Then she locked up the quiet, unlit house. She backed out of the long driveway over a dusting of new snow, glimpsing the park across the street in her rearview mirror. Moms often pushed their kids in the swings there, but on that morning the play equipment sat frozen and barren.

Across the mountains, roads were clear and dry. High desert lay like a canvas of raw sienna under cerulean blue. True drove all day, musing to herself, not even playing the radio. Before dark she reached the Arizona state line, which she'd crossed before but never in winter. Night was coming, taking forever to fall in the expanse of open country. A billboard showing red-and-orange replicas of The Mittens in Monument Valley read, "Leaving Navajoland." No billboard followed to tell her what land she'd just entered. Instead, a small wooden sign pointing left simply read "First Mesa" in stenciled letters.

She turned. Beyond a series of washes and valleys, a pale, titanate moon rose from behind an edge of tableland. She drove toward the growing brightness on a rough road that narrowed to one lane hewn in rock. A few signs too dark to read in the moon's backlight stood along the shoulder. She motored past them, topping the mesa near a neighborhood of ancient pueblos.

The road became a mere path between rows of adobe homes. True's car was the only one up there, moving or not. Low-roofed, dark-porched earthen houses threw blocks of night shadow, their small windows glowing with golden light. No streetlights broke the night, but in her headlights True saw a migration of people. There were pods of teenagers on the move, couples arm-in-arm, families with small children in tow, fathers holding infants, mothers taking their daughters by the hand—a hushed flow of community. True inched the opposite direction, jostled in her wagon by ruts and sudden potholes, aware that heads turned as she drove by.

Too self-conscious to stop, she continued beyond the village to the edge of the mesa. There she killed the car engine and stared at the incandescent sky. Out her windshield, the mesa ended at a carbon void. Somewhere below lay the dark desert floor. In her rearview mirror, she saw only the windows of light cast by the pueblos and a growing gold-ochre radiance in the center of the village.

Her body ached. She felt off balance and ill. Too tired to investigate the glow and too curious not to, she unbent herself from the car. People still streamed past the stone buildings, heading for the light. She joined them.

A drumbeat pulsed, growing louder, drawing her to a stone arena a hundred or so yards in diameter. A bonfire blazed in the center. The enclosing rock wall opened on one side to a flight of steps covered by seated people. Other villagers ringed the arena. True stood with them, the only pale-skinned face she could see in the crowd. They noticed her, she was certain, but their gazes didn't fall on her for long.

The fire's brilliance reached far overhead. On the opposite wall, an elder kept a steady drumbeat with a strength surprising to True. He wore his long, white hair rolled up and bound with a strip of turquoise cloth—a style she recognized from ancient photographs. Catlike, he crouched in a stance so strong it threatened to launch him at any moment from his drum and the wall. He rocked, and the crowd rocked with him. They were individuals but also merged, as water droplets unite in a pool.

In a moment a string of men shuffled into view, hands to shoulders chain-gang style. True counted twelve dancers, aged from their teens to perhaps seventies. Their cotton shirts and pants looked soft and home sewn; their turquoise headbands seemed torn from the same cloth as the drummer's. They quickened their step to match the beat but even so appeared subdued, as if they'd been dancing all day, or all their lives. They kept their faces neutral, as blank as fresh-stretched canvas.

People came and went from the gathering, acknowledged by nods from their neighbors. True watched their easy familiarity with a mix of creeping jealousy and fatigue. Ill again, she left the circle, sure she would heave the little food she'd eaten on the road. Finding a juniper, she bent close and waited. She took in its fragrance but felt too sick to find it beautiful. Nothing came. She returned to her station wagon and laid out her bedding in the back.

Doug would love it there, she knew, fond as he was of high places. He'd pitch the tent near the edge of the mesa, arrange their sleeping bags just so, and make sure they were zipped together and warm. They'd talk until their words slurred about everything they'd seen that day. Then True would curl up against him all night, belly to back, legs drawn up.

But that night she lay alone, planning what she'd say when she called him the next morning.

The last time she'd been pregnant, he'd told her, "Things are just taking off for me at Snow Eagle—I'd never be around to help." True had agreed they could try again later. That was before she knew how sterile she would feel within the clinic walls and how big a void the vacuum tube would leave.

The heartbeat of drumming from the arena lulled her. Minutes later the chatter in her mind ceased, allowing a deep, undisturbed sleep.

In the morning True awoke with a gnawing hunger. The land stretched in all directions, as bright as flames. She rose feeling disoriented. Driving back through the village, she was relieved to draw little attention, passing only a woman wearing a Ganado red shawl pulled close against the west wind. Descending the same road she'd climbed the night before, True observed hand lettering on the roadside signs she'd missed in the dark: "No vehicles past this point—Hopi Village Cooperative." Hot embarrassment rose up in her.

At the base of the mesa, she found a small café. She parked and left her car near a side entrance marked simply "Hopi Silversmith Guild." Just past the door stood a glass telephone booth. She shut herself in it. Dialing from memory, she paused as something shifted in the pinyon and juniper forest—maybe

17

a large animal, running, dodging the sagebrush and trees. She held her breath. It was a creature headed True's way, moving among the sparse desert foliage until it emerged not ten feet from the booth.

It was a young man, naked above the waist. His face and torso were gessoed white. He wore a long loincloth over skin pants and a beaded sash that whipped with his stride. His black, blunt-cut hair was held in a turquoise headband resembling those worn by the dancers and drummer the night before. As the runner disappeared through the door to the guild, True spotted his scarlet athletic shoes with crisp neon-green logos.

She left the booth and followed him in, jostling a rack of bells over the door. Inside, she felt an immediate flood of heat from a fireplace across the room. There was no sign of the running spirit. A middle-aged Hopi man with black-and-silver hair stood in an island of glass jewelry cases, wiping the counter with a white cloth. "Good morning!" He smiled. "How are you today?"

"Dizzy." She staggered toward the fireplace. "I just need . . ." A soft couch provided a landing for her heavy fall.

True woke to the sight of four heads hovering above her. She wondered for an instant if she'd passed on, and this was a welcoming party of loved ones who'd gone before. Her great-grandmother Truella would be there, along with Grandma Betsy and Grandpa Ed, and her childhood dogs Benjamin and Freckles. But wait—the faces came into focus, and she realized these weren't her relatives and long-deceased pets. They were strangers. Their tan skin was burnished with the glow of wind and sun. Among them was the man who'd greeted her from behind the jewelry counter.

"She's coming to," said a massive tribal policeman in sunglasses and dress uniform. A radio receiver crackled on his belt.

"Move back and give her air," said the jewelry man.

A woman in a Ganado red shawl—the same one True had seen on the road?—commanded, "Johnny, go ask Cook for a Number Three plate. And water. Bring water."

One of the faces departed, the one that hadn't yet spoken. It belonged to the youngest of them by far—teenager, probably—with wide eyes and combed-back hair still wet from showering.

The red-shawl woman said her name was Louise.

True whispered, "I'm Truella. Or True."

"Beautiful name. Family name?"

True nodded.

The woman smiled, showing a mouthful of even teeth. "I'm named for my ancestors, too. I have their clan name. Sun Clan."

True let her eyes close. She didn't open them again until the smell of fried meat and burnt sage woke her. The faces were gone, but a T.V. tray sat before her, laden with breakfast. In a rush, she consumed it all—blue corn pancakes with syrup, a generous serving of sausage, and two glasses of fruit juice. When she'd finished, her gut felt full and at peace. She stood and stretched.

True wandered to the glass cases. Rows of silver bracelets and necklaces lay in velvet-lined trays, and the jewelry man worked behind his counter, writing on a notepad.

"Thank you for helping me," she said. "I haven't been well."

He looked up. "Not everyone feels okay all nine months. I know. Louise went through it five times."

True's cheeks deepened to quinacridone pink.

"Don't worry," he said. "Every time, she said it was worth it." He took her hand. "I'm Henry. Where are you from?"

"Utah. South of Salt Lake City."

"Your husband is with you?"

"He's home . . . he's working." She kept her eyes down.

"Ah." Henry released her fingers and pulled a bracelet from behind glass. "Look at this." He ran a finger along the overlay design in the silver band: concentric circles, open on one side, with a many-legged figure in the center. "This pattern is a *kiva*. It means both Home and Place of Emergence."

"Emergence?"

"Creation. Birth. Our elders say we entered this world by way of the first kiva, the *sipapu*. Three worlds before this one failed."

"What went wrong?"

Henry lowered his voice. "Same old, same old. Arguing. They couldn't work things out. Our people decided to start over, so they followed Spider Grandmother up through the sipapu into a better world." He tapped the figure on the bracelet.

True nodded. "I've heard about the sipapu. From my sister, R.J. She works on the Colorado River in the summer."

"It's a sacred place."

In a moment the wide-eyed youth returned, carrying a pitcher of water. "Dad? Mom's busy in the café but said to bring this."

"My son Johnny," said Henry. "He's my youngest. Just finishing high school."

Johnny left the pitcher with his father and turned to go. Maroon letters across the back of his white T-shirt read, "Flagstaff 20K. Peak to Creek Challenge."

"He's still growing," said Henry, pouring a paper cup full of water. "Luckily he's found the Running Way. Got first in his age group in that Flagstaff race last month. He's learning the old dances, too—learning patience. He'll need it when he has a family of his own."

Johnny waved away his father's words as if swatting a fly.

Henry shrugged. "It's the truth."

Johnny rolled his eyes and left the room. As he did, True looked for running shoes on his feet. They were bare.

Henry put away the kiva bracelet. "He says he's too young to think about having a family. Maybe so." He slid the case closed. "But our children are why we live. Even when they give us trouble. Take Johnny. Louise and I thought we were going to lose him a few years back. He went off with some so-called friends, not from the village. I think he wandered far from the mesas. Maybe even got into drugs."

"You don't know?"

"No. Drove us nuts, not knowing. We wondered why we ever had a son, too much heartache and worry. Then Johnny took up running." Henry lowered his voice. "Maybe to impress some girl? Anyway, next he found the dances—rain dance, snake dance, clown dance, corn dance. All of them. Anything to do with the tribe and our clan he got into in a big way."

The jewelry and trays blurred in True's sight. "Earrings," she murmured. "Can you show me some earrings, Henry?"

"Sure." His fingers went straight to a pair of post earrings with matched black curls on disks smaller than dimes. "Here. These are our symbol for water. Waves for flowing around anything in your path. Water is very female. Strong and wise."

"Beautiful. You made them?"

"No. Cecilia did, my oldest daughter. She's getting good— she'll keep the Sun Clan work going long after I'm gone."

"I'll take them. And another pair for R.J."

True dialed the telephone outside the guild. Doug answered. "Hello?"

She opened her mouth to speak.

"Anyone there?" he asked.

She held her breath. Her heartbeat drummed in her ear. Static ticked in the lines that crossed the hushed desert she'd driven alone. Ranges of mountains and a chain of narrow highways stood between her and home.

"True? Is that you?"

"Yes," she said. "Yes, it's me. Me and my baby." She returned the receiver to its cradle. Exhaling, she steadied herself against the glass of the booth.

In the bright morning, the desert looked calm, endless. She stepped away from the shadow of the guild. As she crossed the parking lot, she felt strong and wise, patient enough to flow on her path. She slid in behind the wheel of her wagon and started the engine. She drove south, through a valley where two farmers bent to their hoes in a cadmium red field. Crossing a trickle of water that glinted in a sandy wash, she made her way up and above it. Downshifting to climb the steepening slope, she continued on the ramp of road toward open sky.

Seven Pieces of Pineapple

June 8
Flagstaff, Arizona

Trip arrived here a half day ago. I thought he'd be under his truck in Angels Camp forever and get here late. But I pulled in after sundown and found his blue-black pickup (with new clutch now, I guess) already lined up with a bunch of other cars near the warehouse. His kayak hung out the back of his truck like a big board of lumber.

I tossed my gear under a pine in the middle of the yard to claim a sleeping spot. Just then Trip walked up. He told me the boatmen were in the house. "Let's knock on the door, Mare," he said. I was beat but said okay.

Jimmy the manager opened the door a crack. Out poured light and heat. Trip tried to slip in, me behind him. I saw one of the boatmen—sunburned cheeks, shoulder-length hair, bandanna headband. He smiled with big teeth. I smiled back. But Jimmy did not smile. He told us to come back later, after they'd finished debriefing the latest river trip. We were dying to go inside and sit by the woodstove. It's chilly here, six thousand feet in the air. Hard to believe we're so near the Grand Canyon, the mile-deep furnace.

Outside, Trip swore and pulled out a smoke. "How's it feel to be a flunky, Mare?"

"Different. Who'd you see inside?"

"Lawry. Wesley. Bryce. Big Dan."

"Wow. The legends."

"Yeah," said Trip. "The goddamn elite." He laughed his wicked laugh.

"What about that guide named R.J.?"

"Nope, no women in there."

With the cigarette on his lips he tossed the kayak out of the truckbed so he could sleep back there. He didn't ask me to join him—finally taking no for an answer? I headed for my sleeping bag.

Trip got here by driving straight through, stopping only in Vegas to play blackjack. I came by way of Owens Valley. Sagebrush, mountains east and west, gray swath of highway. Hot, eye-watering winds. Outside Bishop I gassed up at an old station with two rusty pumps.

Some people were gathered at the empty lot next door while the Inyo County sheriff looked on. He told me they were filming a Western. "Andy Griffith is the star. Hang around, you can probably meet him."

"No thanks. I'm trying to beat a friend to Arizona."

"Some friend." He looked inside my VW. "I wish I had a beautiful wife like you who can drive. And a stick shift at that."

His big gold wedding ring caught my eye. "Your wife can't drive?"

"No way. She lost her nerve years ago." Now he does all the driving for both of them.

I continued on—first to Flagstaff to meet Trip and pick up some river gear, then to Utah in convoy with him for our river season. My VW shuddered with every passing truck, made worse by the kayak on my roof. I had to stop a couple times to steady myself. No wonder, then, that Trip got to Arizona first.

June 9
Flagstaff, Arizona

This a.m., up at dawn. Still ungodly cold. I walked a dirt road to the prairie to look for black antelope. The boatmen said you can spot them out with the light ones, running in herds. Black antelope are rare—you have to be patient to see them. Red soil, yellow pine forest. I saw no antelope of any color before hunger pangs hit.

<u>BREAKFAST</u>
granola
raisins
almonds

have bowl
need spoon
need milk

Heading back I stopped at a small house with a sign advertising fresh milk. I knocked and met a lady who keeps cows. She wore an old dress and sweater, had only a few teeth. Her husband sat in a wheelchair watching TV. Some people called the Johnson Sisters were singing about having a friend in Jesus. The husband grinned at me and nodded. Can't speak much, it seems.

He's a shut-in but the wife gets out. She takes a truck and chainsaw to the mountains when they need firewood. She doesn't see the black antelope "but once or twice a year."

Their house sits right on the Santa Fe lines. Trains shriek by day and night. In the middle of our talking, a freight screamed past. The wife stopped mid sentence and smiled as twenty or more boxcars rumbled by. Then she started right back up, asking about the Grand Canyon and the Colorado.

I told her it's got big water but I haven't been down it yet.

She grew up in Salmon, Idaho, by the Lemhi River. "It's shallow all summer, full of these rocks." She held up a jar crammed with round river stones. All sizes, all colors. "I was like you back in my twenties. Big blue eyes. Blonde hair, too— but mine was long, down my back."

She asked me to bring her more stones from the river. "Any river will do," she said.

How she keeps herself from hopping a freight out of there I don't know.

Back at the warehouse, Trip was hanging with the Canyon boatmen. They thanked me for the milk and stood around eating cereal from plastic mugs. Bryce asked about boating in Utah.

I told him I hear it has beautiful canyons but I haven't been in them yet.

"You'll get there," said Big Dan. "By the way," he asked Trip, "how'd you get your nickname?"

"He fell over the port-a-potty one night last summer," I answered.

The boatmen roared.

Trip glared at me over his cigarette smoke. "I'd *had* too

many beers." Like that was better than just not seeing it in the dark.

We helped the boatmen pack for Lee's Ferry. Wesley was binding the ends of some tie straps, so Trip pulled out a Bic lighter to heat-seal them one at a time. Seeing it would take forever, I opened up a cookstove and portable propane and sealed a half-dozen straps at once. The boatmen stopped what they were doing to watch until Jimmy the manager showed up and told them to get back to work.

Now the river truck is loaded with rafts, oars, lifejackets, and food boxes for 14 days on the water. Tomorrow we'll convoy up to Lee's Ferry at dawn. The Canyon boatmen will ride in the truck, Trip will haul the raft and other gear we came for, and I'll drive my VW with Trip's kayak tied next to mine. Detouring to the Ferry was his idea. He wants to "get in good with the GC boatmen" so they'll ask him to work down here.

Bad idea, I said. We have to pack out the first Green River trip day after tomorrow.

He said, "No sweat. We can drive straight through." He raised an eyebrow. "Don't forget who won the race to Arizona."

<u>DINNER</u>
peanut butter
no jam
potato bread
green apple
oatmeal cookies (6)

June 10
Lee's Ferry, Arizona
Spectacular! Or should I say Grand? Today the water in the

Colorado is a startling, teal-wing blue. Contrasted with purple and pink cliffs to the north and — wow! I get it. I could see working here forever, even though the Lee's Ferry boatramp is mobbed, the rafts are heavy (one ton unloaded), and everything's so hot in the sun you can't touch it. The boatmen move their gear with channel locks, including these *mondo* chains and angle iron on thick plywood decking that would be overkill on a smaller river. All on a stretch of pavement the size of a Kmart parking lot.

Trip and I helped the boatmen pull all the heavy stuff around. It was insane. I had an idea and told Trip, "I'll lend the boatmen my kayaking gloves. They'd work better than their crazy channel locks."

"Right." Trip grabbed my gloves. "I'll take those to Lawry."

Trip was back with the crew in a flash. Typical. My idea, my gloves, and Trip taking credit. In a huff I pulled my kayak down from the VW and paddled upstream toward Glen Canyon Dam. The river is slow up there and quiet, a good place to think in private. I stopped on a large chunk of rock in a stretch where big domed couches of sandstone reach between river and sky. Six snowy egrets. Handful of ravens flew past in a burst—noisy! I calmed down and fell asleep on the warm rock. After the sun dropped behind the cliffs, I woke up and paddled back to the ramp.

The boatmen were standing around Trip and slapping him on the back. He had on my gloves. The others were wearing those white cotton ones like you get at Ace Hardware.

"Hey, Mare," said Wesley. "Your friend here saved our asses." When Trip had showed Lawry my gloves, the other boatmen remembered the cotton ones Jimmy had bought them for rowing.

"Great idea." I glared at Trip.

He narrowed his eyes back at me. I wanted to whack him with my kayak paddle but in my newfound peace from napping

I knew that would only make me look bad. Instead I asked for my gloves back. He made a big show of taking them off and returning them to me like I was the jerk here.

The boat ramp quieted down for the night. Rafts from other companies were lined up along shore. Boatmen spread out to the campsites to cook their dinners. Bryce told me 200 people will launch from here tomorrow. Most will go in motor-powered rafts, huge Army-surplus pontoons that make even our oversized oarboats look tiny.

River gods help me—I want this place.

Same day. Midnight. Writing by flashlight.

After rigging, the boatmen ate a steak dinner courtesy of Jimmy and his chain-smoking assistant Bob. They'd driven to the boat ramp to help but arrived after the hard work was done. Dark was coming. A single great blue heron flew by with silent wings. Trip and the crew huddled in crumpled poses like the truly tired. Jimmy asked Trip to share in their dinner because he'd helped so much with the glove idea. Fine. I put my kayak back up and got out the makings for a peanut-butter sandwich. Head boatman Lawry called me over for dinner.

"There's plenty," he said.

And there was. What a spread: steak, rolls, salad, corn on the cob, fresh pineapple. I went over and dug in.

Jimmy and his sidekick Bob sat off to one side, talking. Bob puffed on a cigarette the whole time. Jimmy watched me as I licked pineapple juice from my fingers. Next thing I knew, he pulled me aside.

"You know, Mary," he said. "You were welcome to the dinner."

"It's Mare. Thanks, it was great."

He went on, "But there were only *seven* pieces of pineapple.

Just enough for the main crew, Trip, and Bob and I."

He had to be kidding. I smiled. But Jimmy did not smile. Trip was eating pineapple across from me, looking worried. Thinking I was beating his time with the Arizona boss?

"So what should I do?" I asked Jimmy. "Cough it up?"

He stormed away and drove off in a van with Bob the cigarette puffer. Where to? To report me to the rangers? When it seemed he'd left for the night, the boatmen came alive, second wind I guess, congratulating me for getting rid of Jimmy. They passed around a box of wine marked Day 12 in black felt-tip pen. A few swigs and I felt a hand on my arm. Big Dan feeling my biceps!

"Keep rowing, Mare," he said. "You'll get hired here."

Trip snorted. "She'd have to be stronger than that."

Bryce laughed and lifted his own skinny arms. "It's not all about muscles. We have one woman, R.J., who does it with smarts."

Lawry said I should try for it. "The Canyon's the best."

BEST

rapids: Lava Falls (says Bryce)

sidecanyon: Havasu Creek (Lawry)

mudbaths: the Little Colorado (Wesley)

wall: Nankoweap (Big Dan)

sunsets: West rim (all)

The boatmen went on: the longest trips, the most money, the best canyon, the funnest rapids. All the women you could ever want, or men in my case. And parties every night!

We raised our cups. "Every night!"

Later I headed for the restrooms and Trip followed. Maybe to ask for the thing I'll never give him? But he said, "I am *going* to get hired here."

"Me, too."

"You?" He laughed and walked away.

It's true women are scarce. But I have to go for it. Otherwise, you know what they'll say. Same as the poor sheriff's wife.

June 11
Vernal, Utah

Lordy, lordy. What a day—ten hours of following Trip's truck to Utah. Now in the Vernal KOA, surrounded by horse trailers and pickups. There's a rodeo this week. Aspiring cowboys on the road with their parents. We're drained and obnoxious. We have to get some sleep before packing for the Green tomorrow a.m.

<u>BREAKFAST</u>
Cheerios
milk
bananas (2)

My first views of Utah: rock walls, little stream valleys, aspen, cottonwood, fir. Who would've guessed? Big conifers on the ridges. We sped by. Trip insisted on stopping at Texacos—he says his truck runs only on their gas. At the Panguitch Texaco we lunched on sandwiches and watched the locals.

"Something not to be missed," said Trip.

Man on a bay mare in front of Smith's supermarket, talking to a smiling cop. Kid with a 1950s brush cut, holding pop bottles, waiting to cross the highway. High-school girls with pigtails in plastic ball ties, running from their car to the store, then back.

"I'll be damned," said Trip, sucking on a cigarette. "Must've crossed a time warp at the Arizona line."

Arizona, Arizona—everything went bad in the end.

June 12
Vernal, Utah

RIVER FRUIT SALAD
10 apples
6 apricots
6 peaches
grapes for 22
canned pineapple

This a.m., writing out shopping lists for the Green River. Good to be back at work but hard to be away from every boatman's dream: rowing the Colorado farther downstream. No sooner had I thought that than a long-distance call came from Jimmy saying one spot is opening up on the Grand Canyon crew. He asked Trip to transfer down there. My heart dropped about three feet.

Trip noticed. "Give up, Mare. You might as well settle in up here."

"And why is that?"

"You know you'll never get hired in GC. The water's too big for girls. The boats are too heavy. And you didn't exactly hit it off with Jimmy."

That all's supposed to stop me?

RIVER FIRE BOX
charcoal & lighter fluid
oil
black pepper
strike-anywhere matches

Hot day in Vernal. Cars creeping by on Main. Men in jeans, cowboy hats, and long-sleeved shirts even in the heat. Maybe not so hot to them. Born and raised here? Boatmen from other companies walk by in shorts and t-shirts, ammo boxes in their hands, buck knives strapped on their belts. "Beehive State" (for industry) on every license plate.

We packed rocket boxes in the grocery store parking lot. Trip came across the fruit I'd bought for the fourth night's salad. "What gives with all the pineapple, Mare? Ten cans of it? Three would be plenty."

"We won't want for pineapple on this trip."

Trip's been talking up the Canyon to the Utah boatmen. They barely listen. On the way to put-in, Miles read a paperback and ignored the talk. Snake, who was driving, said he likes it here.

Trip laughed. "Not me. I'm going to transfer to the Canyon faster than you can say 'Jack Mormon.'"

Acres and acres of alfalfa in the valley. Land fenced for quarter horses. Thunderheads blooming over the mountains, and sego lilies flowering in carpets of white. We crossed little creeks and farm ditches and almost got to the river before we blew a tire.

Snake pulled over. Miles and Trip blocked the wheels and

jacked the right rear of the van. Frozen lug nuts. Across the highway was a little garage. I went in. I bought soda from a vending machine and borrowed a can of WD-40 from the mother of the mechanic.

She asked about the rivers we'd be running. I said I'd heard they were wild but hadn't been on them yet.

Back at the van, Miles sprayed the lugnuts with the WD-40. They came right off. Good thing—Trip was already red in the face from trying to loosen a couple.

The air smelled sweet from new things growing. I bent down to pick up an old river stone, round and white, half the size of my fist. It shone like a mirror when I rubbed it clean. Opal? I'm keeping it until I get back to Arizona.

With the tire changed, we crossed the bridge over the Green. Swallows dipped near the water. A wedge of geese passed overhead. Heading south? If so they'll get to the Canyon before me. But I'll keep rowing, like Big Dan said. Maybe I'll get there slow because it's a man's world and Jimmy doesn't want me. But all paths lead downstream when you follow the river every day. That, and when guys like Trip tell you to settle in.

The Middle of a River in Flood

If Gwen could see the river tonight, she'd see it's not wild and rising hard, like that day ten years ago. No, the water below Half Moon Bar is smoother than a stream cobble. When the river's quiet like this, you can believe trees never slide by, big and torn up, rocks still in their roots. You can imagine the whole old flight of steps leading to the lodge never gets pulled up, folded, and tucked away like a ladder, so high the water won't carry it off. Tonight the river's tame, reflecting a big moon. The breeze up the canyon smells fresh and clear, not thick with mud, the way it smelled the time we tried to run the river in flood.

Gwen of all people would notice the peace tonight. When I got back today after her memorial, I chopped wood until dark, bit by bit splitting the oak rounds that remained from last year. As I worked, I thought of her lying there in the hospital, how weak and shrunk up she'd looked. Damn, the doctors—did they do any good? Seems their treatment amounted to no more than bailing a big river with a bucket. The cancer left nothing, barely enough to bury.

Near the end of my wood-chopping, when I was tired but

still swinging hard, sending chips flying, I missed the splitting stump and just grazed my left boot. That scared the hell out of me, so I had to take a break. I walked down to the water to sit on the steps until I stopped shaking. I pictured the younger Gwen, her face when she finally knew we were in trouble and both struggling to catch air.

That morning of our river run, she and I drove to the boat ramp in the dark. She was the girlfriend of Ryan, Half Moon's caretaker, and she wanted a lift downstream to see him. She trusted me to be the one to take her. "He says you're the best, R.J.," Gwen said, when she first called to ask for a ride.

"Thanks." I did have the years at it, on rivers all over the West. "Tell him we'll see him at the lodge."

As we followed the river road, Gwen noticed the madrones in our headlights, wet from the weeklong rains. "What's that shimmering?" she asked.

I leaned close to the windshield and looked up. "You mean the madrone leaves?"

"Yes! That's it—all silver in the lights. They're beautiful, R.J. Magical."

Gwen's green eyes glowed like the undersides of the leaves. Her face looked pale and bright, a headlight of its own. She fixed on the trees as she held a thermos cup of hot tea in her small, pale hands. They were wrinkled and years older than her young-woman face and its smooth skin. She turned the light of her eyes toward me again. "I see why you and Ryan love it here. It's gorgeous!"

We were towing my brand-new driftboat. I'd painted it up in town myself—four coats of sky-blue paint on the wooden hull, black trim on the sideboards, hand-lettered name on the stern, *Sayonara Too*. I'd never even fished from the boat; it was that new to me. I'd bought it to enlarge my fleet that for years had consisted of a single aluminum driftboat, *Sayonara One*.

A pair of newly varnished ash oars fitted to brass alloy locks completed the *Too*. It was perfect for chasing down salmon and steelhead and running guests to the lodge. Getting to Half Moon would be a breeze in that rig.

When we arrived at the Grave Creek boat ramp, the river looked higher than the phone report had said. The feeder creeks must still have been pumping in runoff that the depth gauge in town hadn't measured. Gwen and I stood at water's edge, in our slickers and woolies and milking boots, and watched the muddy flow.

Something else was unexpected, even besides the water level, and she put her finger on it. "There's no one here. Do you think we'll have the river to ourselves?"

"No, we're just early. Someone's bound to launch later." In truth, though, I'd never been alone at that boat ramp, no matter what the hour or weather.

"It's fantastic—all wild and empty."

The water was bigger than we ought to run alone. But Gwen said, "Ryan told me you're the only one to ride with in high water."

I nodded. It was true: big rivers had become my specialty. The belief we'd be okay on that flood, that most of the rapids would be washed out, started to take root in me.

We backed the trailer down to the shore, though we didn't have to back it very far, since the river covered half the ramp. Then we lined the *Too* into an eddy, loaded a bit of gear for overnighting at Half Moon, and parked the truck and trailer up by themselves in the big lot. I ran through the standard safety talk—lifevests tight, throw line ready—then took the oars. We kicked off from land and whipped into the current like a leaf in the wind.

Gwen sat up front, braced on the gunnels with her mittened hands. The river surged down the middle in one good set of standing waves. High water covered most of the rocks. From time to time she looked back at me, smiling and big-eyed. Sometimes surprise side rollers hit the boat in the belly or caught the sharp rails at the bottom, a feeling I never liked much considering how easily those driftboats flip. But Gwen didn't know—she just laughed.

"Is it always this exciting?" she asked.

"No, not always."

"But it is now. The river's alive!"

About two miles down from Grave Creek, the rain started again. Gwen noticed something strange—all the tributaries pumping in dark water from the side canyons.

"What's different about the creeks?" she asked. "They're not muddy like the river. They look like tea. Or coffee."

Dark, leaf-stained water poured from gullies and swirled into the foamy current. With the ground already soaked up, little canyons normally choked with gooseberry and fir flushed and spilled that darker color. Most hadn't run that hard in years. Scary to me now, the thought of the creeks churning in from places we couldn't see. Back then, though, I didn't think. I just struggled like mad to control the boat.

The huge falls at Rainie had washed out, an easy channel of small swirling waves. That was no sweat, although it spooked me to glide over a ledge of rock, normally so tall above the river, buried under tons of water. At Horseshoe Bend, the current shot like water from a firehose through that U-shaped curve, then climbed the bank as far as I've heard it does when the gauge reads twenty feet. That was more than twice as high as had been reported that morning. And in Mule Creek Canyon, the river reached clear to the top of the gorge: surging, pushing, roiling up in boils. I'd have given my spare oars to know the gauge reading then. It was higher than I'd ever seen, higher by far than anyone runs solo. I didn't say anything to Gwen, so of course she got me for being quiet.

"Everything okay, captain?" she asked.

I didn't answer. I was listening.

"R.J.—"

"Shh."

Gwen turned to me, surprised. Then the question left her face, because she heard something, too. Something like a train coming from a long distance, or a jet thundering. Or every last bear out in the woods growling. But it wasn't any of those things. I knew what it was—rapids. Big rapids. Above a certain size they lose their friendlier white noise and take to roaring. Maybe they become all water and no air, and the rumble fills the sky and shakes your ears and heart. The sound meant that downstream, not quite around another bend, was some big whitewater. Blossom Bar in flood.

Gwen looked startled, maybe because there was nothing to see. Blossom bellowed below us, but just the lip of it showed. I could guess what was down there: rapids filling the rock garden and covering the marker boulders so they were just muddy humps. From up top we could see only a bowed surface of river rolling ahead.

The only thing to do was pull to shore. I rowed so hard to get over, I almost overshot a little rock cove I was aiming for in the right bank. We made it in, though, and I pulled close to a cliff where we moored the boat. My hands shook as I tied up the bowline while Gwen waited. Then we kind of tiptoed downstream to scout Blossom.

"Good God," I said when I saw it.

The rapids looked huge and ugly. The usual house-sized boulders were under water, and they made nasty reversals that kicked up froth and spit like I'd never seen before on this river. The standard run, where you swing wide to the left and cut back hard right, was not the usual highway. Not nearly so. Rowing the normal route would mean pulling through some rowdy water and around two mean sucking holes.

Gwen watched me as I watched the rapids. "Why's this so much worse than everything else?"

"Blossom's got the biggest rocks on the river, for some reason."

She thought a moment, then asked the million-dollar question. "Can we do it?"

"Well, I've run stuff this bad before," I said. But I never had when there wasn't another boat downstream ready to bail me out.

She kept looking at me, just waiting, I guess.

"We could walk from here," I said. "It's only two miles to the lodge." But we were on the wrong side of the river—we'd have to line the boat back upstream about a half mile before rowing across. The thought scared me: two of us lining there, with all the fast current and slippery rock. "Or we could hike out to the road." Ten miles farther on the river path. We could make it, but well after dark.

"What should we do?" asked Gwen. Her face was bunched up with worry, and I wanted her to stop looking that way. I thought of the *Too*, so pretty, bucking at its mooring upstream. Overnight like that, it might bash up. At least if we made it through the rapids and got to Half Moon, Ryan would lower the steps for us. We'd secure the *Too* with guy-lines and rest easy in warm beds.

"Let's go," I said. "It's just two good pulls."

Her face lit up. "Outstanding."

I checked the straps on her lifejacket. "Remember. Keep your feet downstream if we land in the river."

She giggled, but with a nervous edge.

I peeled off my heavy clothes, a habit I'd picked up on trips running big rapids, but I decided to keep on my rubber boots. Gwen chose not to strip down—she was cold enough already, she said. She just sat on her haunches on shore, one hand holding the bowline, waiting for the signal. I stepped into the boat. From my seat at the oars, I listened to the river's roar and strained to see my entry into the spray, shock waves, and foam.

"Okay, Gwen!"

She stepped into the bow, carrying the line with her. We swept into the current. I rowed left with everything I had, reaching far ahead of me, finishing each stroke with my legs. She watched downstream, her hands gripping the gunnels. I made the quickest, strongest strokes possible, arching all the way up as I pulled, recovering as fast as I could. Even so we only reached mid-river by the top of the rapids. The current was just too much for me—something I hadn't felt before, not even earlier that day. As we closed in on the lip of the falls, she got a good look downstream. She turned and screamed, "Pull, pull!"

The big pyramid rock loomed to our left, just a tip of granite in a huge mound of brown water. We made a last-minute punt and ran a chute between the pyramid and the gorilla-faced rock. Dropping over a little falls on the downstream side, the boat made a sickening, scraping sound. Still, we landed straight, even though it was a hard fall that popped the oars from their locks.

"Shit." I slammed the oars back in place.

Gwen still held the gunnels. "We're okay! Pull! Pull!"

I pivoted to the best angle I could and rowed, but the upstream rail of the boat caught in a surge that spun us. We washed down toward the Volkswagen rock, just a monster midstream hole at that water level. The *Too* dropped nose first into the hole and stopped, but only for an instant before shuddering, snaking up, and twisting over on top of us.

I've always thought that life's like the river, but anybody can see that. There are backwaters and shallows, bridges and dams. There are smooth parts and rough parts. Like Gwen's illness, years after the river run—that was a rough part. When she lay there, in the medical center that had held out all kinds of hope, I asked her.

"What's it feel like, Gwen? A bad swim?"

Her skin was so pale, I could see into her. And her bright green eyes had turned golden and keen, maybe from the pain, maybe from morphine.

"I mean you being this sick," I said. "Does it feel like you're drowning?"

She thought about it, her face bunched up. "No," she whispered. "Much worse. Stronger." She fell asleep, and as usual I sat with her until she woke up.

She meant worse than feeling a wooden boat crash onto your back in the middle of a river in flood. She meant stronger than being sucked straight down by the water in your boots— worse than staying under so long and tumbling around so much you doubt you'll see daylight again. Or worse than swallowing enough water to make you heave, with no one waiting to pick you up.

Gwen's swim was bad, worse than mine, maybe because she'd kept on her heavy wool clothes. When my boots finally tugged off and I shot to the surface for air, I saw her floating low and fast, going farther downstream every second. In a minute, speeding ahead like that, she'd be swept out of sight.

I swam as hard as I could to get her. When I caught up, it was only because she was stuck in some whirlpools along an eddy fence, wheeling like a spinner cast out for trout. She churned the surface with her arms, looking too weak and lost to find shore. Her nose was red, and her hair hung in her pale face.

"Swim, Gwen! This way!"

As I reached for her, she looked around but not far enough to see me. A current shot her back out into the river.

No, I thought, I can't go out there again. I'm not strong enough to get her.

Then I saw it—an oar sliding by, fast and sleek, out in the river. It looked so streamlined that I knew what to do. Pushing out and swimming low and hard, I told myself to go like the oar. I strained and shoved and broke through each wave, never taking the long ride over the tops, but slicing straight through them, just like a ten-foot, solid-ash oar.

Gwen's head showed up downstream past dozens of curlers. When I closed in on her again, she was swirling on the eddy fence of another backwater, floating even lower than before, swallowing water. Then the swift current headed upstream caught her.

"Gwen! No, stop!" She was about to wash out the top of the eddy.

But I got her. With my right hand, I grabbed for her lifejacket, pulling her back from the whirlpools and main current. With my left I reached for shore, finding something thin and tough hanging in the water from the muddy bank. It was a tree root, sweeping along in the water—one of a mass sticking down into the current where soil had washed away. It didn't feel like much, but it was enough.

I dragged us over and helped Gwen struggle up the steep bank. Out of the water, we huddled together on a little patch of slicked-down grass, gasping and coughing. When I looked up, I saw the *Too* across the river, just passing the surging eddy below Half Moon Bar. I could only stare. The boat looked like a big fish come to surface, turning in the current, heading fast toward Four Mile Canyon. I had to sit and watch my prize roll out of sight when I wanted so much to run along after it, to do something, anything. But I sat next to Gwen, holding her hand, and didn't move.

"Thanks, R.J. You saved me."

"The hell I did. I about killed you."

"No, you saved my life, so let me thank you."

"Okay."

"Thank you."

When the river looks peaceful as it does tonight, sometimes I forget how it can rise up brown and pushy. Half Moon's steps are lowered to the water, easy to reach. But on that day, the lodge might've been on Pluto for how hard it was to get to. Across the river, not far from where I pulled Gwen out, there are trees on the bank—Doug-fir, big-leaf maple, madrones—with their roots hanging down toward the water. They're far above it, of course, with the river so low.

Gwen and Ryan split up years ago, and he moved to town. The lodge's owners let me stay here anyway and help around the place between trips to the hospital to visit Gwen.

The last few months watching her, I felt helpless again. Hours and hours, days and days, sitting and holding her old, wrinkled hands. Her veins by then were easy to see, and her skin had been wounded by needles. She'd collected more colors of bruises than I'd ever seen, even on people who'd broken bones or taken bad falls.

I'd hoped that if I held her hand long enough, or just right, she'd have cause to thank me again. But of course it didn't go that way, and in the end all her words were gone.

I could sit by the river and stare longer, but I'll probably go split some green rounds, just for something to do. I'll have to be careful, though, not to miss the stump again. No doubt I'll still think of Gwen lying there, and of me holding her small, weak hands in my stronger ones. That's all I could do. There were no tree roots to catch hold of. Her life had gone on to surgery and radiation and chemotherapy, things I know nothing about—nothing like boats and currents and how to fish the steelhead that run in the fall.

Weaker than Water

Good God, R.J.! Look at the size of that wave.

It gets like that. When the river's high. Like a mountain of water.

Holy bejesus. Bigger than a mountain—it's higher than K2. A planet.

They must be letting monster flows out at the dam.

The whole river pours through that thing. Where are we supposed to run?

Start center, pull right. Only way to go, Mare.

What? Hang it out there with that wave ready to eat you?

Yeah. You have to start in the middle and pull right. After you pass those holes over there.

You can't get left?

No possible way. Not with that boat-sucking eddy over by the wall.

No lie. I wouldn't want to be anywhere near that wall. You ever been over there?

Once. I just squeaked left of the wave.

Far left?

Uh-huh. But it was really low water—not like this.

This is unbelievably high water.

Yeah, Mare. Un-fucking-believably high. Way higher than it's supposed to get anymore.

But it's only water, right? Nothing's weaker.

Yeah. It can only kill you.

Gracias for the reminder.

De nada.

What's all that wood, R.J.? In the eddy surge? Can you believe the amount of wood in it? Big old logs.

Driftwood the size of pontoon boats.

I thought wood that big didn't get down here anymore.

It doesn't. Can't get past the dam. That's got to be old wood from above the high water line.

Right, R.J. Way up there?

Has to be. From up in the damn talus.

So how high did the water get, do you think?

Well, hell. It was fifty-eight thousand and rising this morning. Must've gotten over sixty thousand to float that wood.

God. And we thought twenty thousand was high.

Yeah. But it's three times higher today. Look over there, Mare. The boulder bar's all under water. The willows have washed away, gone on down the river. And look—the old path is covered. We can't walk the people around on it. They'll have to take the high road.

Maybe I'll take it with them. I mean, what are our options?

I'm telling you. That middle-to-right run. There's nowhere else to go.

But what about that channel farther right, over the bar? Could you cheat through there?

Mare. No possible way. I've been there. It's floor-rip city.

I'd rather rip a floor than flip out in that wave.

Believe me, I know. But then you'd be sunk.

But that wave! How tall is it, R.J.? Forty, fifty feet?

At least. I've only seen it taller one time. In the early eighties high water. It flipped a thirty-three-foot motor rig end for end. Like a rubber ducky.

You saw it?

Yeah. The wave stood the rig up and surfed it. The water looked twice as tall as the boat—like seventy feet. The boat fell back on itself, on everything—frames, boxes, people—right on top of them.

What? That never happens.

Never, but it did then. And the scariest thing was hearing it. *Ka-whomp!* Like a tall building fell into the river.

What'd you do?

What could we do? We radioed out for help and ran down with all the safety lines we had and . . . hey, Mare, I probably shouldn't be talking about this today.

Probably not. Go on.

There were floaters everywhere—people in the worst of it, people washed downstream. Some stranded on rocks. Down there, all along shore. Some had been trapped under the boat and were scared shitless, just waiting. Took us a while to get everyone out.

Were they hurt?

Some. No drownings though. A miracle.

What'd the motor boatman do?

Quit that day. On the spot. He rode a Park chopper out and

never worked another trip. I heard he moved to Phoenix and got a job in real estate.

God, R.J., can't say I blame him.

Hell, no. But these things happen at high water. Trust me. I know. Besides, it wasn't the worst thing I ever saw here.

Why? What was?

Years ago. I was standing on this same rock, talking to a private boater who said he'd run the river for years. Older fellow who called himself the Old Man of the River. That motor flip had just happened, and smaller boats had been going over, too. The river had dropped some, but it was still high and we wanted to quit our jobs every time we saw it. The wave looked sort of like it looks right now. Anyway, the Old Man was right here, and he was smiling.

How could he be? I mean, God, R.J., if it was like today . . .

Yeah, it was. I told him the wave had been eating boats. I told him experienced guides had been portaging their trips—rafts, coolers, kitchen boxes, everything.

What'd he say?

Nothing. That's just it, Mare, he didn't say a word. He just smiled and showed no fear. Then he got out there in his little boat—it was a fifteen- or sixteen-footer—and sure enough he couldn't make the pull. He got swept sideways to that wave and flipped.

No! He swam? Anyone with him?

No. Just him. He'd walked his one passenger. He washed through rest of it and on downstream—must've been in the river five miles before we pulled him out.

You pulled him out?

Me and a guy I worked with. We jumped in a raft and pushed out after him.

Did you catch him?

Yeah, but only after he'd turned blue. He must've drowned in the first mile. But that's just a guess.

God, R.J.

God is right. Nothing like seeing the dead empty look of the Old Man of the River. Took a lot of whiskey to wash the taste of him out of our mouths.

You CPR'ed him?

Yeah. For hours. And after that and a flip of my own up in Oregon . . . well, it took me a while to want to come down here again. And I've never cared for high water since then.

Like today.

Uh-huh. Just like today.

But you're here.

Yeah, Mare. I came back, and I've been here ever since.

Right. Where else would you go?

Like I said. There's nowhere else *to* go.

True Minds

Frank used to snore like a weed whacker, he told me, but had to lose the habit in Southeast Asia. The Navy SEALs trained it out of him, he said. Before serving three tours in Vietnam, he used to wake even himself up with the racket. "I was obnoxious, Mare. Couldn't shut up to save my life. But now—negatory. If I can stay quiet, anyone can." He didn't say much else about his time in Special Ops except that his patrol worked best between midnight and dawn. That's when they slipped into villages and huts to slit the enemy's throat. "Three a.m.," he said. "Nobody can stay awake then. Not even the baddest-ass guys."

"God, Frank. What a nightmare."

"Yeah. It sucked. But it's not the hardest thing I've ever dealt with."

"What was?"

"Being home. Trying to be normal."

He kept to himself so much, I assumed he'd have no trouble staying quiet about our affair. "You won't tell anyone, will you, Frank?"

"Of course not. It's just between us."

It was a first for me, sleeping with another woman's man. On our river trips, I'd slip into his tent after dinner and out before nightfall. We were keeping it secret—that and a piece of hidden treasure I'd discovered at River Mile Seven. I'd found it while freeclimbing alone on limestone, casting around on the wall, just playing. I was sort of heading for a cave about thirty feet off the ground. Pulling myself up the rock, I peered into the dusky hole. Something was in there, an object about the size of a basketball. As my eyes adjusted to the dark, the phantom form took shape.

It was an ancient water vessel. It had to be a thousand years old, left by the long-gone people whose dwellings and rock paintings were scattered throughout the river canyons.

"Mare! Dinner!" Frank called from the beach near the rafts. His voice sounded small across the distance. Could he hear my heart pounding from that far away? Not much escaped him.

Resting my hands on the cool clay of the vessel, I tipped it toward me. The coiled surface bore row upon row of an early-style corrugation I recognized from photographs. A crescent-moon crack broke the lip. Inside were a few shriveled spiders, wispy strands of cobweb, and a pinch of plant seeds. The surface of the vessel felt brittle and hard, more like metal than earth.

"Mare!" Frank called again.

I replaced my find and climbed to the ground. A soft sand path led back to camp. I vowed to tell no one—not the passengers, not the other crew members, and above all not Frank.

But after dark in his tent, he kissed me, his musky skin and soft mouth clouding my thinking. Fifty feet away, river current sighed on an eddy fence. "So what was up there?" he asked.

I got out of my clothes. "Up where?"

"In the cave."

He ran his hands over my naked belly. As my mind went warm, I let slip my secret: the patterned clay skin, the tiny pack-rat treasures inside. "I've always dreamed of finding a whole pot," I said. "Not just shards." I rubbed the hair on his chest. "Ever see one?"

"Once."

"And you reported it, like a good river guide?"

"Hell no."

"Then what?"

"I hid it better." He yawned, my cue to go.

I unzipped his tent door. "Frank? You won't tell anyone?"

His breathing had already deepened. I leaned close to the tent and listened, but there was nothing to hear.

Days later, off the river, Frank found me at the boathouse repairing a worn raft tube. He informed me that his wife, Emma, wanted to meet me for lunch. As I listened to him, I put hand pressure on a neoprene patch I'd just slapped over a layer of contact cement and abraded fabric. Then I asked, "Did you tell her about us?"

His dark eyes smoldered. "She guessed."

"Oh, right."

"Damn it, Mare, she's my wife! You've got to help me."

"Help you what?"

"Save my marriage."

"Fine time to be thinking about that." I knocked over the toluene jar with one awkward slap of my glue brush. Thinner soaked the newspapers on the floor, and the stink of solvent filled the air. I stormed out of the boathouse, glancing back to see Frank's reaction. He'd dropped to his knees. He was cleaning up the spill.

Two days later, Emma called me, voice trembling. "I was a river guide, too, you know. Before I married Frank."

"Where?"

"Here. Like you. But I got pregnant with Becky." She paused before continuing with a statement that sounded rehearsed. "I should get to know you better. Frank thinks you're so special."

Not feeling very special, I agreed to meet her downtown. I drove to the Travelodge café as thunderheads above the La Sal Mountains creased the sky with lightning. A rain wind blew through my summer clothes.

Reaching the café, I almost ran into Emma, also on her way in. Her eyes poured out hurt—a lot like Frank's eyes, come to think of it. Her full head of auburn hair and smooth skin looked perfect, well cared for, not like my skinny brown ponytail and nose peeling from sunburn. She was gorgeous. What the hell is wrong with Frank? I wondered.

She chose our table, then unfolded her linen napkin and smoothed the tablecloth. She ordered white wine; I asked for water. As we studied the menus, she spoke without looking up. "When he admitted he was seeing you, I wanted to leave him. It's too much to go through. Again." Hand shaking, she drank, then set down her glass. "But why should I leave? Really, why? I still love him. Our daughter loves him."

My appetite was gone. Still, my Monte Cristo sandwich arrived without delay—a mass of bread, ham, and powdered sugar. With the first huge chunk in my mouth, I felt like the snake who swallows too much and has to digest for a week.

Emma poked at her chef's salad. "You know, I'm mad at you." Her fork thrusts into the lettuce looked more and more savage. "It's hard enough to keep a marriage going without someone coming along to sabotage it."

I nearly spit out a mouthful of half-masticated Monte Cristo. What had Frank told her? Obviously not that he'd made the first suggestion. Not that he'd tapped on the zipper of my tent after midnight near Brown Betty Rapids, wanting "to talk." Or that he'd shaken me from sound sleep at Dark Canyon to say how much a part of him I'd become.

"But we'll be fine," Emma said. "We always are. I just wonder how you'll be." She leaned toward me—just a bit—across the table.

I sprang out of my seat. Throwing down a twenty, I left her and bolted out the café door. The thunderstorm had settled in, with veils of raindrops already washing dust from the sidewalk. Ducking under a store awning, I held my car key and trembled.

Go ahead and rain, I thought. Storm. You can't get into a certain limestone cave down by the river. You can't so much as move an ancient thread of cobweb in the shelter of the canyon.

That evening, my friend Jane joined me at the Poplar Place for a drink. "So he told his wife." She tapped a cigarette before lighting it.

"No—she guessed."

She snorted as a cocktail waitress brought us each a Sunrise.

"Come on, Jane. That's what he told me."

"And we have every reason to believe our precious Frank."

"Jane!"

"Well, hell, Mare. Aren't you angry?" She squinted over her cigarette smoke.

I drank, shuddering at the strong taste of tequila. "More like hurt."

"Huh." Jane pulled an ashtray toward her. "Why not quit him?"

"I can't. Frank doesn't exactly take no for an answer."

"Have you ever said 'no'?"

"No."

She arched an eyebrow. "So it's that good, sleeping with a highly trained murderer?"

"Jane . . ."

"Okay," she said. "But face it, Mare. He won't leave his wife and daughter."

Blood crept into my face. "New subject, please."

"All right." She swept back her shoulder-length ebony hair. "Well . . . my photography business is booming. I have a new show opening at the Main Street Gallery."

"Great!" I signaled the waitress for two more Sunrises. "To celebrate." After toasting Jane's show and draining my drink, I leaned across the table. "Have you ever seen a Pueblo pot in the wild? Right where an ancient one left it?"

"No! Where?"

"I can't tell you. Only Frank and I know."

"Why Frank? Was he the one who lent you a raft to run your private trip? Did he forward all your mail when you lived in Oregon?"

"No. It was you."

"All Frank's done is cheat and lead you on. Come on, you can tell me. Really, no one can keep a secret like old Jane."

Someone was feeding the jukebox again. The tequila filled me with vertigo, and I began to sway to Tina Turner. "Okay," I said. "You promise?"

"Mare! Wake up! Listen to this!"

Heart pounding, I sat up. "Jesus, Frank." A bright sweep of stars lit the moonless sky. "You scared shit out of me."

"Sorry." He knelt in the sand beside my sleeping bag, wearing a headlamp and holding a spiral-bound stenographer's notebook.

"What time is it?"

He checked his diver's watch. "Fourteen hundred. Two a.m."

I lay back down. "Aren't you an hour early?"

"Not funny. Mare, listen. This is us:

"Let me not to the marriage of true minds
Admit impediments. Love is not love
Which alters when it alteration finds
Or bends with the remover to remove."

"I like that—'true minds.' What is it?"

"Shakespeare. Sonnet 116."

"Wow, he wrote that many?"

Frank didn't make a sound, but he laughed so hard his shoulders shook. Tearing the page from his notebook, he handed it to me with only the slightest rustle. "This is how our love is."

I propped up on an arm to see the page and his tiny scrawl. "What about Emma? What about saving your marriage?"

"Oh. Yeah." He turned off his headlamp.

"Good night, Frank." I dropped back to my pad.

A moment passed. He sighed. "It's a beautiful night. In a few minutes the moon will come out."

I sat up again. Across the canyon, reflected light crept along the wall of rock—first just a sliver of brightness, then a wedge, then an entire sheet of radiance. Down the beach, toads bleated like small sheep. The air smelled earthy from a breeze blowing up the muddy river.

Frank said, "That whole wall over there is going to light up like a pumpkin."

"You mean jack-o-lantern."

"Right." He put an arm around me, and we lay down together. Whispering, he stroked my hair as I drifted in and out of sleep. "We are true, you know . . . you and I . . ."

That night I dreamed about my hidden treasure. Moonlight didn't reach into the cave. Wind blew but didn't rock the vessel—it stood as motionless as any other bit of stone in the canyon walls. In the morning, my final thought on waking was of old, expert hands smoothing wet clay. Brown fingers pressed a bone shard again and again into the pot's pliable surface. The soft strains of a wooden flute mixed with laughter from the pueblo.

I opened my eyes. Sunrise hovered in a strip of light over the east wall. Frank was gone. He hadn't left even an impression in the sand beside me.

As we floated past the cave on the next few trips, I scoped it with binoculars. Nothing seemed different or disturbed. Summer shifted toward fall—marked by muted light and cooler mornings. With the shorter days of mid September on us, I tried not to think of the coming winter. I packed food for our last trip, humming as I filled the waterproof boxes.

Frank pulled up in his van as I was locking the warehouse for the evening. Keeping the motor running, he rolled down his window. "Mare, I have to talk to you."

"Where's Emma?"

"Back at the house with Becky. Get in."

I climbed in and slid toward him across the seat.

He stared straight ahead. Driving south out of town, he followed back roads east of the highway. After some false turns and backtracking, we ended up on the road to the dump. We passed bulldozed mounds of old appliances, furniture, broken toys, and ripped sheets of plastic. Ravens rose up crying from the red dirt, and the sweet smell of decomposition filled the air.

Frank stopped the van near a heap of tumbled earth. My voice came out shaky. "Are you going to dust me? Throw my body in the dead dog hole?"

"Damn it, Mare." He whipped off his sunglasses. "The office knows."

"About us?"

"They're saying you won't have a job next year. Plus you've been dropped from next week's trip."

"Dropped? What about you?"

He looked at his hands.

"Frank? It's just me?"

He kept his eyes down. "It's the pot. It's missing."

"Missing?"

"Yes, missing! Or course, missing. You are so naïve. Everybody found out about it."

"How? It turned into a regular sideshow attraction and you didn't tell me?"

"Word got out. You didn't know?" He laughed, a short, angry sound.

"'Word got out'? That's it?"

He stared into the distance as late-summer raindrops sprinkled the windshield. "I do love you. That will never change."

"Shut up, Frank." Bolting from the van, I stumbled toward the nearest pile of earth. There were decomposing bags with unknown contents and the stink of death. My feet sank to the ankles in soft soil as I stopped short of some rotting animal. I screamed and scrambled to run, but Frank caught my T-shirt from behind. He reached an arm around me but didn't draw me close as he guided me like some invalid back to his van.

"Jane!" My mind swirled. Frank and I'd parted with few words, cut off as I slammed the passenger door on his last claims of undying love. "Jane!" I ran up the stairs to her studio. Out of instinct, I reached into my pocket for a key but found only Frank's sonnet: "Let me not to the marriage of true minds . . ." I balled it up, jammed it back in my jeans, and swung open Jane's unlocked door.

"Jane, you won't believe—" Something on her desk stopped me. There among the catalogues, notebooks, and correspondence sat a dozen or so eight-by-ten, black-and-white photographs of a Pueblo pot. Stunned, I flipped through the images. They were all of a corrugated vessel with a crescent-moon crack. The object was arranged on black velvet, surrounded by shining, polished turquoise stones, and posed next to spiky foliage and broken rock near a river beach. I carried the photos with me as I burst into Jane's darkroom.

"Mare! Close that door!" She held a dripping print with metal tongs. "What's wrong with you?"

"Oh, come on. You know."

She wiped her hands, and we both stepped out into the hall. Reaching for the photos, she said, "Easy! You'll wreck the finish."

"Fuck the fucking finish. You promised."

She opened the top drawer of her desk. Finding a pack of cigarettes, she pulled one out. "I just went to see it."

"But it's missing!"

Her dark eyes widened before she looked away.

"Who'd you tell?" I asked.

"Me? I just caught a boat to the beach at Seven Mile, took some pictures, and hiked out."

"Who took you down the river? Frank?"

She shrugged. "We put it back."

"Where is it?"

Her eyes teared. She held the unlit cigarette between her first and second fingers, like she was flipping me off even as she trembled. "You're to blame, Mare. Not me, not Frank, not Emma. You." She turned, stuffed her cigarette in a mug on her desk, and rushed to the wooden staircase to the street. I ditched the photos on her desk and followed. After two blocks of trying to catch her, calling her name, I stopped.

The smell of early snow swept from the mountains. Jane's figure grew smaller as she fled.

Plunging my hands into my jeans, I found the crumpled sonnet. Frank was no doubt at home now with his wife and kid, a fire in the woodstove. He'd be packing a few things for the next river trip before going to bed and lying in Emma's arms. Silently.

A gust of cold wind snatched up the poem. I ran after it, whimpering as the wind carried the words out of reach. People hustled by, pretending not to see or hear, collars raised against the cold. The words disappeared up the street, and I ran after them—first sobbing, then cursing, then falling silent before I gave up the chase.

A Real Café

You may think someone's your opposite—neat where you're messy, tough where you're tender—until you run a river with him. Then as you're getting through rapids together, working long days, watching each other's backs in all kinds of drama, you get to see all the ways you're alike. Take Jack and me, for instance. When we first met, I found him as serious as sunstroke. He was all protocol on our raft-patrols of the winding canyons of the Yampa River and the deep, red gorges of the Green. Our jobs as backcountry rangers required we run week-long trips in silver army-surplus boats heavy with supplies: canned goods for the field stations, bags of powdered lime for the outhouses, picks and shovels for trail work—you name it. If it was needed for Park operations at the river campsites, we carried it in a couple of government-owned rafts named *Chub* and *Humpback* for the endangered fish that lived in those two rivers.

Jack and I had come to the job on different paths. He'd been a ranger in various parks since college; I'd been a whitewater guide working farther downstream. I didn't share the details of why I'd switched to rangering—no doubt he'd find me unworthy enough without learning the sordid details of my previous life.

Our disparate appearances vouched for our different backgrounds. My park uniform was likely the most crumpled set of gray-and-greens in all fifty states. Jack, however, seemed to know from experience how to keep pressed creases in his sleeves and standard-issue slacks. Likewise my short hair stood up uncombed and wild, while Jack's stayed groomed and in place beneath his mesh ballcap. I wore drugstore sunglasses from off the rack; he alternated between designer-frame prescription shades and spotless wire-rimmed readers.

"Pardon me, Mare," Jack said one time when we stopped for lunch. "But do you know Laura? At headquarters? She works for Interpretation."

"Yeah." I'd met her. Laura spoke with a charming Georgia accent and moved with grace and liquidity. She gave polished presentations to the hordes of visitors who flooded the interpretive center, her manners smooth, her long, dark hair falling from her shoulders as she reached for the binders, pens, and papers that were her teaching aids.

Thinking of that flowing hair, I felt for my own and found mostly exposed neck.

"She wants to come on one of our trips," Jack said.

"Oh?" I spread a cracker with peanut butter.

"So? What do you think?"

"Well . . . " I chewed my lunch. "She's cute, Jack. But can she dance?"

Because Jack could cut a rug. He loved to go to town on Friday nights after we'd reached the boat ramp at take-out, deflated and rolled the rafts, and driven back to headquarters. He danced as if he were born to it, his dips and spins infused with a rare grace. At the urging of any music, any time, he came alive—a dream in sneakers.

A few times, Jack danced with me, who loved old disco films and knew some moves of my own. In his arms my funky improvisation fit his ballroom style like leotards. He twirled and tossed me away just to reel me in and toss me again. He lowered me until my spine brushed the floor and sprung me, weightless, back to his chest. Somehow our different approaches meshed, but, because Laura was watching, he seldom danced with me. During "Park Nights" in town, he preferred to sit beside her on a folding table near the wall, swinging his legs to the music—but not dancing.

One lunchtime off the river, we cruised in his green Ford truck to the Burger-Freeze for shakes and fries. The truck had no radio, so Jack kept an old tape player on the seat between us, snapping his fingers to vintage Sam Cooke tunes. "Know this one, Mare?"

I shook my head. "That's pre disco. Before my time."

We sat under the awning at the diner, Sam Cooke still with us but playing low, and watched tourists pass on the interstate. When the burgers arrived, Jack said, "Oh, by the way. Laura's coming on our patrol next week."

I sucked air into my chocolate shake. "Why?"

A blush crept into his cheeks. "To . . . learn about the park, of course. She can't get time off for the whole thing, so she's hiking in to meet us at Jones Hole."

"Fine."

He squinted at me through his glasses. "You don't like her."

"Like her? I love her. Come on, Jack, you're wrecking my lunch."

He punched a button that silenced the music, and we passed the rest of our break without speaking.

Near the end of our next river trip, Jack and I stopped at the Echo Park field station to resupply with drinking water. We always topped up there before starting the six hot miles to the Jones Hole river campground. As we pulled into Echo, Jack filled the air with Woody Woodpecker laughs. His voice bounced off the opposite cliffs and through the vast space between the canyon's sandstone walls. The air reverberated with the call of one woodpecker, then two, then three. He giggled until his hazel eyes spilled tears and, reaching to wipe them, he caught sight of his watch. "Jeez! Laura's probably at Jones by now. Let's skip the water."

"Not get water?" I waved him off. "You're nuts."

"Come on, Mare. We can fill up at Jones."

Gathering the empty water jugs, I started toward the station. "You go ahead. I'll catch up."

"You'll follow me?"

"Right."

"You'll follow me?"

"Yes!"

"Better not, Mare, I'll call the cops." He giggled again.

"Just go."

He hesitated but only for a moment. As I settled the jugs around the station's hand-operated pump, I watched him row downstream as a cat watches birds out the window—curious but detached. When I launched a half-hour later, I took my time, letting my oars dangle in the current, leaning back on my rowing seat. Thunderheads built to the west, growing like fast-blooming flowers. At Stateline Rapids, I waved to the battered sign marking the edge of Colorado. Three bighorn sheep nibbled on penstemon in the north wall. "Eat, drink, and be merry," I said. "Tomorrow you may be in Utah. With *Laura*." The sheep gazed at me with goggle eyes before lowering their heads again.

At Jones Hole, I found Chub barely secured to an undersized piece of driftwood. "Great, Jack," I said to the empty beach. "Now I'm sure you've lost your mind."

Unpacking a safety line, I strung both boats to a sturdy park service stake farther from the river. Then I rummaged through the provisions we'd brought for the Jones Hole ranger we called Dan-the-Man. To myself, I sang, "Cookies, bananas, apples . . . cookies, bananas, apples," as I tried to gather all the food as well as the other supplies—spare batteries for Dan's radio pack, inflatable splints, and new filters for his water purifier. It was obvious there was too much to carry and I needed his wheelbarrow. With a small bit of the fruit, I headed for his cabin, which was hidden a hundred yards off the main trail behind a stand of cottonwood and box elder.

Near Dan's place, the hypnotic rustle of green boughs stopped me. Mesmerized, I stared at the trees, becoming aware of soft laughter beyond the rustling of leaves. I tiptoed nearer the cabin. Soon I made out the distinct sound of voices and the sight of Dan's big hammock swaying on the porch with the weight of two people. A woman laughed. In a voice dripping with Georgia sweetness, she said, "Picky, picky. Where do you get your notions, sugar?"

A man giggled. I knew Jack's laugh, and this wasn't his.

"What sleazes," I grumbled as I turned back to the main trail. "Sleazes." I broke into a run. "Sleazes!" I shouted, rounding a bend full steam and nearly crashing into Jack.

"Whoa, Mare!" He laughed. "Who are you talking to?"

"Nobody."

He was sweaty and covered with dust, his uniform shirttails as I'd never seen them—rumpled and hanging outside his shorts. He eyed the bananas in my arms. "Why are you carrying those?"

"Just bringing a handful while I get Dan's wheelbarrow. Where'd you go?"

Jack removed his cap and brushed back his damp hair. "To the rock art at Ely Creek. Dan-the-Man said he'd had a report of some vandals up there. I ran up to have a look."

"See anything?"

"No. The rocks look fine."

"Figures."

Jack eyed me. "What's that mean?"

"Well, why didn't Dan go himself?"

"He said he'd be right behind me with the radio pack." Jack wiped his glasses. "Funny thing. I never did see him. Maybe we missed each other at the Ely Creek turnoff. No big deal. I'll go get his wheelbarrow."

"No!" I shouted. A bunch of bananas fell to the ground.

He reached down to pick them up. "Mare, what is wrong with you?"

"I can get the wheelbarrow. I have to . . . take him this fruit anyway."

"Okay." Jack shrugged. "I'll go clean up at the river. Laura's supposed to be around here somewhere."

Back at Dan's, the hammock hung empty. I snuck toward the cabin. Luckily there were no signs of life except for a few flies buzzing. I left the bananas on an orange-crate table on the porch, then found the wheelbarrow and aimed it toward the water. I stopped short when I saw Jack looking hangdog, standing by the boats.

"Jack?"

"I found Laura."

"Where?"

"The far end of the beach. Wrapped around Dan-the-Man."

Parking the wheelbarrow next to Humpback, I waited while Jack stared at the water. After a minute, he said, "Huh. She never let on."

"That kind never does."

I climbed into my raft. Picking up two spare battery packs we'd brought for Dan, I hurled them into the wheelbarrow. Next I flung the case of water filters, then a Number Ten can of *Western Family* pinto beans. As supplies hit the steel with thuds and clanks, I threw things harder. Jack watched open-mouthed as I lifted a flat of eggs over my head.

"Mare, wait! Don't break those!"

I lowered them. "You're right."

"Here." He took the flat, carried it to the wheelbarrow, and, just when it appeared he would ease it down, lifted it head high. "A pox on both your houses!" He slammed the eggs onto the can of beans.

The wheelbarrow fell over. Everything spilled. We both admired the destruction.

"Wow, Jack." My heart soared. "It's a mess. Let's leave it for them."

We coiled the bowlines, pushed our rafts into the current, and rowed through Greasy Pliers Falls. We floated onto slower current as the sun set over multihued cliffs downstream. At a camp called The Cove, we cleaned up, cooked a pot of spaghetti, and drained three beers apiece.

"I wonder what Dan-the-Man thought when he found his stuff?" Jack asked.

"Undoubtedly the work of the same vandals who ruined the petroglyphs." I tapped my third beer against Jack's. "*Salud!*"

He giggled. "Bet he's mad as a wet hen." His smile faded. "God. What does she see in him?"

"Oh, Jack, you're too good for her. You follow me?"

"Yeah."

"You follow me?"

"Yeah!"

"Better not, Jack, I'll call the cops."

He was still laughing as he walked through the darkness toward his sleeping bag. I was left to listen to a flock of Canada geese across the river and to stare at the crisp, full Milky Way.

The next day, Jack and I took off the river at lunchtime and bolted for headquarters. We drove south on the highway, continued east past the Burger-Freeze, and stopped under a canopy of cottonwoods shading a real café—an indoor restaurant with two-page menus, bottomless mugs of coffee, and leatherette booths. We parked among the pick-up trucks lined up outside the windows like horses at a saloon. Inside, we ordered chicken-salad sandwiches and orange sodas, avoiding the weary eyes of the other customers, men from nearby ranches or the oilfields south of town. They sat without speaking, appraising us in our sweat-stained park uniforms and silty tennis shoes.

A jukebox stood silent in the corner. "You know," whispered Jack, pointing with his thumb. "It's still three-for-a-buck here."

I pulled some coins from my pocket. "Will you dance?"

Looking around the room, Jack raised an eyebrow.

"Okay, okay," I said. "I'll play something anyway." At the jukebox I chose a few songs I recognized, then scanned the labels for one more tune. I punched a third button, the only one with a handwritten name: "Beautiful Body, Bellamy Brothers."

When the music started, I raised my soda glass. "This one's for Jack." His blush began before the Bellamies were even through the first verse of "If I Said You Had a Beautiful Body, Would You Hold It Against Me?"

My face warmed as the play on words hit me. But my red cheeks had nothing on Jack's. He turned nearly purple as he checked the room for gawkers then stared at his plate. There was nothing for me to do, either, but keep my eyes to myself until the song ended.

That evening at dusk, as I hung my laundry from the trip, distant Sam Cooke tunes drifted through the housing compound. Jack, his wet hair combed back, was crossing the parched lawn outside his apartment. He saw me and stopped. I pinned up a T-shirt. He opened the door to his truck. I hung and smoothed a pair of wet jeans.

He spread his arms wide, showing off his fresh cotton shirt. Overhead, bats fluttered after insects in the fading light. Jack waltzed, hand to his belly, in that style that I knew fit mine so well. When he mouthed, with obvious exaggeration, "You follow me?" I nodded, waiting.

Then he dropped his arms, laughing like Woody Woodpecker—once, twice, three times—before stepping into his green pickup and slamming the heavy door. He pulled onto asphalt, where his truck tires hummed toward the music and dance floors of town. His taillights burned red and receded beyond the sage and rabbitbrush, far past the bend in the road where the river sweeps south.

Sandstone

The paleontologist taught Erv that bones in a river settle parallel to the current. Erv hadn't figured that out, though he'd worked at the quarry for twenty years before the paleontologist arrived, green as corn, from Yale. It took Erv some time to get over his first impressions of the man. For good reason. For one, Dr. Case *ran* from the housing area to the river every day— rain, snow, or summer heat. This was years before joggers were as common as beehive license plates in Utah. Evenings as Erv headed back to town, he passed Dr. Case running along the quarry road in shorts, sleeveless T-shirt, and tennis shoes. Dr. Case called running his meditation.

"You mean medication," Erv said, thinking of the pills Betty took to relax when she was his wife.

"No, Erv. Meditation."

It was the first time Erv heard that word used outside of church.

Another reason: the paleontologist socialized with the river rangers when they weren't on patrol, having them to dinner, going on outings. Those two, Jack and Mare, laughed like jackalopes in heat, as if they'd caught the giggling disease while boating the Green River. Erv found Dr. Case's interest in recreation beneath a man with a doctorate in science. Erv scratched his graying head over that one.

Until Dr. Case showed Erv that the rock he'd been digging was old river deposits and the bones lined up the way the current left them, Erv didn't see the connection between ancient streams and the modern rock. He had noticed plenty about the bones he'd been finding at the quarry all these years, though. For one, he knew they showed up in little piles—or big piles, seeing that they were dinosaur bones. For another, most of the long bones—femurs, tibias, fibulas—lined up west to east. Erv knew it all meant something, but his job was just to dig.

He'd been hired at the quarry and had worked there forever, in spite of not having a high-school diploma or formal training. He knew his way around a rock bar and sledge and how to use the fine tools, too. And he could handle a jackhammer at any angle, which came in handy for the big finds. No wonder he was good—he'd started in the gilsonite mines when he was sixteen. His dad had left home, and though he wasn't ready to, Erv had dropped out of high school to work full time. When he got the quarry job years later, he learned to detail the bones right where they lay, with ice picks and soft-bristle brushes. That was the meanest work, the hunching over with tiny tools for hours at a time. It just about did in his back and legs. Still, he outlasted the whole string of supervisors who ran the quarry for years before the paleontologist came along.

Sometimes when Dr. Case was running, his young wife, who'd also gone to college, followed along pushing their infant daughter in a stroller. They were out there even when afternoon winds blew up the river and kicked up dust and little bits of rock. Couldn't have been too good for the baby, and Erv wasn't sure what the wife got out of it.

One thing that rankled him, because he grew up Latter-Day Saints, was that Dr. Case used to invite in the missionaries just to argue with them. He'd studied the Book of Mormon enough to figure he'd found the loopholes, and then he asked those kids into his home and debated their faith. He teased about Jehovah, who he called the God of the quick and the dead, and he got a big kick out of the Land of Moron and the angel Moroni, who led Joseph Smith to the golden tablets. Those things didn't seem funny to Erv, and he sure never questioned them. But he resolved that a man of science can't be called on to trust in the church or mysteries of the spirit.

At work, Dr. Case got to watching Erv and naming everything. Erv would clean off what he knew to be a shoulder bone, while Dr. Case put on his goggles and said, "Look, Erv, *Apatosaurus* scapula." Or Erv would finish with a string of tiny neckbones that Dr. Case called "cervical vertebrae from a juvenile *Stegosaurus*." Erv liked hearing the fancy names, and he surprised himself by remembering them. Sometimes, though, Dr. Case would hover, saying Erv should use a smaller-sized pick, or a bigger one if he thought the work could go faster, or that it was time to clear away the debris. Then, one day, he said, "Careful, Erv, you'll gouge the socket."

"I know it, sir. I'm being careful."

"Shouldn't you be using the number six pick?"

"Believe me, Dr. Case, I've done over a hundred ribs this way."

"Maybe so. But let's get this one right."

That did it. Erv peeled off his hardhat and safety glasses. He dropped the pick, walked past the office, and continued out into the parking lot. Dr. Case followed him all the way, asking where he was going, what he was doing. Erv didn't answer.

Dr. Case dogged him to his truck. "Erv, stop! I didn't mean it. You know me—I'm a paleontologist. I can be boneheaded."

Erv leaned against the bed of his truck and pulled out his smokes.

"Erv, I shouldn't have interfered. You're the expert. I need you on that cliff."

That stopped Erv. He suspected deep down that Dr. Case would do fine if he chose to quit, which he didn't, because he hated like hell to look for work. But Dr. Case was getting on his nerves on the rock. Erv lit a cigarette and turned to him.

Dr. Case's dark hair blew in the afternoon wind. Behind him, Split Mountain stood out in the sun, bright and clean. His eyes looked that deep blue color the river turns late in the afternoon.

"Dr. Case, we've got to get a few things straight. Number one, Jehovah is not the God of the quick and the dead. He's the Eternal *Judge* of both quick and dead."

"Oh, I've been teasing, I—"

"And we say Mor*un*, not Mor*on*."

"Fine, but—"

"And I hate to say this, Dr. Case, but what you don't know about detailing bones could fill your library in there."

Dr. Case stood a minute, squinting in the low-angle light. He stared at Erv, then down at his feet. Finally he held out his hand. "You're right, and I know it. No hard feelings?"

"No, sir, I guess not."

Erv took his hand and shook it.

After that, Dr. Case began to spend more time with Erv, asking questions and telling him things. Erv reveled in the novelty of the talk. He'd never been farther from the valley than Salt Lake City and hadn't had schooling above the eleventh grade when he'd quit to help support his mother, but Erv knew when he found something special. He was the first to point out the almost-intact skeleton of the baby *Stegosaurus* and the crocodile scute nestled behind the *Camarasaurus* toebone. He called the paleontologist's attention to those finds, and Dr. Case put the names to them.

One day as Erv was enjoying a smoke on the cliff, taking a break from handling the jackhammer, Dr. Case sat nearby and dug in the broken rock. "Look at this, Erv," he said. "All sandstone, but all different. Layers on layers of sandstone."

"That's so?"

Dr. Case nodded. "An old river bed. Millions of years of sandbars building and shifting and changing."

Erv pondered that. "But these dinosaurs didn't live in rivers. Where'd the bones come from?" All these years he'd figured the quarry was a swampy place where the big lizards dragged themselves to die, like the elephant graveyard in *Tarzan*. Dr. Case's river theory blasted that idea.

"Carried down from upstream. The *Dinosauria* probably lived and died throughout the basin, and the river in flood picked up their bones and carried them here."

Erv thought a minute. "But bones don't float, Dr. Case."

"No, but they do roll on the bottom. Or they float if they're still in a carcass. And these were likely carcasses shunted into eddies by side components of the main current. Picture it, Erv." He reached out his arms to take in the entire cliff. "A river of floating dinosaurs."

"Ah," Erv said. "I can picture it all right. You mean bloating dinosaurs. You wait until spring—you'll see enough puffed-up cows in the Green to scare you off steaks."

That night after work, Erv walked to the public library to read about rocks. He couldn't get over Dr. Case's new notions, even though he'd been digging on the cliff for two decades. He found three good geology books that he spread on a wooden table near the magazine racks. He read about sandstone, that it forms in rivers and oceans and desert dunes. The rock can be full of calcium or quartz, tough or crumbled, gray or buff. In his digging, he'd felt the changes in hardness, and those were just in river rock. He couldn't imagine how ocean beach or desert sandstone would feel.

On his way out of the library at closing time, full of thoughts of rocks and rivers, he walked smack into his ex-wife near the "Latest Arrival" shelves.

"Why, Ervin," Betty said, hugging a hardbound book close to her chest. "What are you doing here? I thought you'd given up books."

"True. But I'm doing a little research."

Her eyebrows lifted, and her mouth formed an O. Erv saw she was tan and lovely, just the right amount of plumpness in her pink summer dress. Her hair looked grayer but wasn't permed as tight as before. It curled soft and easy around her face.

"You look great," he said, in spite of knowing he shouldn't.

She blushed.

He walked her back to the house, where he'd lived with her for almost twelve years. At the edge of the valley, piles of black-bottomed clouds and short curtains of rain hung over the mountains. The scent of sage blew in from the desert outside of town. He heard soft whinnies from the Searles' horses beyond the high school basketball field and sharp zaps from the electric bug killers in the Rasmussens' garden. As he and Betty passed under the quiet rustling of elms, he told her about Dr. Case and how the quarry was once a riverbed.

"There's sandstone there where a river used to be, maybe even a big one like the Green." She didn't answer, but she was giving it some thought.

At the house, the lawn looked green and trimmed. A single light shone in the downstairs window, where his reading chair once was. He wanted to open the door, walk inside, and sit and read as if time and disappointment had never pushed him from her. Instead he said, "Goodnight, Betty."

He left her in the half-darkness, knowing she was beautiful and tender, but not knowing what to do about it.

In time, Dr. Case lost his pasty grad-school look. Maybe it was his meditation or just living in country with a wide, blue sky. He took up fishing. Every weekend he'd visit Flaming Gorge, or a mountain lake, or some part of the Green. He went after the fish whole hog, like he went after everything. In the quarry lunchroom, Erv found an article Dr. Case had clipped from the *Lavern Express* about Utah's famous, oversized German browns. Fishing catalogues covered the paleontologist's desk. Dr. Case bought hip waders, a canoe, one of those khaki vests with all the pockets, and a hat with a lambswool strip for keeping flies.

"I'm in heaven, Erv."

"No, Dr. Case, it's Utah."

He grinned, and Erv couldn't help but grin back.

Dr. Case was pulling in support for the quarry, too, calling professors and finding money for the digging. Erv realized that a man doesn't get all the way to a Ph.D. in paleontology without a burning interest, and Dr. Case was on fire. He'd travel to conferences in Laramie, Denver, or Las Vegas, or invite guests to the quarry for his talks that earned standing ovations. Every time, Dr. Case gave Erv plenty of credit: "the man who's learned his rocks from the ground up," he'd say, asking Erv to stand, or "the fellow who does all the real work." After a while, Erv got used to it, and he looked forward to going to talks at the quarry and swapping tales with visiting professors. Most of all, he looked forward to going to work.

One afternoon near quitting time, as Erv was using the jackhammer, Dr. Case waved him over. Erv shut down and took out his earplugs. The two men hunkered near a pile of ribs. "Look, Erv, see that little tail of sediment trailing east? That means the river here flowed from the west."

"That seems likely."

Dr. Case pointed to a big femur heaped over with smaller bones. "And this legbone stopped everything else in this pile."

"How so? Like a traffic jam on Main?"

"Right. When one unit stops, it almost always concentrates the others. Or the bones are drawn into an eddy behind a rock. Not a lot of isolated pieces here, are there?"

"No, sir, I had noticed that."

"Well, it's no coincidence. It's physical law." He called the piles "waves," so named by a scientist at the University of California, Berkeley.

Erv climbed to an area of the cliff he'd been detailing. He pointed to two huge sauropod ribs stacked against an end-up vertebra. "Here's another wave, Dr. Case."

"And another," Dr. Case yelled from the top of the quarry, where two femurs, each about five feet long, leaned together easy and neat as dominoes.

"And this is the best one yet." Erv kneeled near a string of neckbones that curved around a nest of skull plates.

"Wait," said Dr. Case. "Don't move! I'm getting my camera." He climbed down the face of the quarry, trotted along a ledge of sandstone Erv had been digging in all week, and stepped off the edge of the rock where the light was dim. He tumbled fifteen feet down the steep path that bordered the cliff's west end.

Erv scrambled to help, but the paleontologist was already sitting up tall, dusting himself off, by the time Erv reached him. "No sweat," Dr. Case said. "Just a little problem with my eyes."

"Sir?"

"I don't understand it myself. Can't see much in the half-light."

"There's an eye doctor from Salt Lake who gets to town once a week, Dr. Case. You ought to go see her."

"I'll do that." He fetched his camera from the office.

The two men stayed at the quarry until well after midnight, logging the waves of bones and understanding for the first time what they meant. "This is it," said Dr. Case, his face weary but his blue eyes bright. "This is the beginning of something. Don't you agree?"

"I sure look at this rock a whole new way."

Dr. Case was quiet a moment. "Erv, I want you to come to Denver with me in September."

It took a minute for that to sink in. "Oh no, sir, I'm no professor. I've never even seen the outside of a conference hall."

"You know more about detailing than anyone I've ever met. You could contribute a lot to the meeting."

"Well, I'd love to, but—"

"Then it's settled. I'll authorize travel for us both." He checked his watch. "Oh, jeez, I'm out of here. Tell you what— take tomorrow off. I'm going to. I feel like going fishing."

Erv agreed to that. He gathered up his things and walked outside. Dr. Case was still in his office when Erv turned from his truck to admire the quarry lights against the Utah sky. Then the big lamps switched off. In the starlight, he saw Dr. Case lock the gate and cross the parking lot.

"Erv? You there?"

"Yes."

"It's a beautiful night, isn't it? I could almost believe there's a heaven up there."

"My heck, you mean you don't?"

"I don't think so—I haven't been able to reconcile religion with my work." He opened his jeep door. "What about you? You quit the church, do you believe in God?"

"Oh, yes, sir. I always have, especially in hard times. The church might've got on my nerves, but the Almighty never has."

"But what about the bones? You understand fossils. Aren't they an indication that life evolves? That Earth wasn't made in six days?"

"Dr. Case, those are the details. I figure the Spirit is big enough to work them out. Or that evolution itself is His doing." The paleontologist was listening, so Erv continued. "To me what counts is prayers. I couldn't have gotten through any other way when my dad left and I had to quit school. Or when Betty and I split up."

There was a long pause. Finally Dr. Case said, "You're lucky, Erv," and waved good night. He drove down the hill—to his wife and baby and their three-bedroom home in the housing area.

Erv stood by his truck a minute. Cool air from Split Mountain washed down around him. Below the light burst of stars, he spotted a satellite on a north-south course. He remembered what Dr. Case had said about the conference and that he'd called him lucky. "Thank you," Erv said to the heavens he knew were up above the darkness.

The phone call from Sheriff Hatch came twenty-eight hours later, when Erv was deep in sleep in his apartment. Erv had spent his day off in the library reading paleontology papers sent at his request from the University of Utah. Toward closing time, he'd looked up to see Betty standing by his reading table.

"Hello, Ervin. You're spending a lot of time here."

"More and more." He removed his reading glasses. "I'm preparing for a paleontology conference in the fall. Dr. Case invited me."

"My. Well, it's good to see you reading again."

He walked her home. They passed lawns and sprinklers and water-filled gutters. At the house, lilacs filled the air with sweetness. The same light brightened the window where his chair used to be.

"Betty," he said. "I'm feeling better."

"I know."

"I'm thinking maybe I can be somebody."

"But, Ervin. You always were somebody. I tried telling you that."

"Uh huh. Drove us both nuts telling me that."

She looked startled, then leaned back and laughed. "Not that you ever listened."

"Well, you know me—too thick to plow."

When he bent to kiss her head, her hair felt soft and smelled of the same lavender shampoo he remembered. Then it was all he could do to step down from the porch, with Betty half hidden behind her front door. But he wasn't ready, so he walked across town to his place. He sat up reading more of the dinosaur papers until midnight. When the sheriff called at five a.m., Erv was still catching sleep after two late nights in a row. He woke with a start.

"Erv? It's Jim Hatch. I need your help. There may have been an accident."

Hatch said he'd heard from Dr. Case's wife: the paleontologist had gone to Flaming Gorge and hadn't come home. She hadn't worried at first, because he sometimes stayed out fishing long past dusk, too excited to quit, and couldn't see well enough to drive until dawn. He always carried a sleeping bag in the jeep, just to be safe. But he had a CB radio, too, and never failed to call in. The wife was beside herself when she hadn't heard from him. She'd asked Hatch to contact Erv.

Rays of sunlight were just touching the mountains when Erv met Hatch and his search-and-rescue team downtown. The men stood in front of the station in their hunting colors, drinking steaming coffee from Styrofoam cups. They rode together in a van to Flaming Gorge. Erv listened to the police radio, its static and garbled messages, and tried to calm his stomach. Hatch asked him some questions, which he answered as best he could.

"What kind of fishing does he do, Erv? His wife said he's got bad eyes—did he tell you that? He's new in the valley. How well do you know him?"

They parked near the dam, next to Dr. Case's white jeep. Hatch guessed as soon as he saw it that no one was inside—the windows weren't at all fogged. Erv wiped a bit of dew off the cold windshield. The mouthpiece of the CB was hooked in place on the dashboard. A sleeping bag sat on the front seat, rolled up in its blue cover. Hatch used a megaphone to call for Dr. Case, with no luck, while the sickening feeling grew in Erv's stomach.

Hatch headed to the reservoir while Erv led a few men downstream.

A band of fog hung on the river. The water smelled fresh and cool. The Green flowed fast and shallow, with narrow eddies. There were sudden deeper spots behind boulders that Dr. Case would have recognized as holes if the light were strong enough.

The first thing Erv found was Dr. Case's plastic lunch cooler, right by the river, with just an apple core and sandwich wrappers inside. Erv called again, and tried to run, but the boulders were wet and slippery. He had to walk instead, near shore with the other men who were calling for Dr. Case. Erv was hoping to spot him sitting up tall, brushing himself off.

Erv did find him. He knew where to look—Dr. Case had taught him. Sure enough, the paleontologist was in the river, his waders full of water. He'd washed into an eddy, where his arms trailed upstream parallel the current in the backwater. Erv pulled him to shore and turned him over. An eerie paleness had settled under his new tan. And his blue eyes—which Erv had figured missed nothing—were open, but the light was gone.

That afternoon he called Betty. She said, "I heard."

They met at the library and sat out back at the picnic tables. The air was full of the sound of cars cruising Main and the smell of fresh-cut alfalfa from beyond the neighborhoods. Erv's stomach hurt the way it had since morning. He kept recalling those young eyes with nothing in them, a sight he wished he hadn't seen.

"He was it," Erv said. "He was the engine. I wasn't ready for him to leave."

Betty picked pieces of cottonwood fleece from the picnic table. "I'm sorry."

"And there'll be no conference now. No being somebody."

She didn't speak right away. When she did, her voice trembled. "I think you're wrong, Ervin. I think he'd want you to go to the conference."

"By myself?"

"Yes."

They sat for a time without talking. Erv was grateful for the silence, which she never used to allow.

After a while she stood and smoothed her skirt. She asked if he'd like to come for coffee later on. Erv nodded. Then she walked home across the big lawn behind the library, arms swinging, flowered skirt swaying. Beyond her, light changed on the buff-colored cliffs of sandstone. Erv couldn't stop staring at them—would he ever? They stood this side of Flaming Gorge, with its legendary German browns and its cold, rushing stream below.

The Road to Bonanza

Antonia's first morning with the driller set the tone for the days that followed. They ate breakfast in separate cafés. They drove to the Green River in individual vehicles, Jet in the charcoal-gray flatbed with mounted drill rig and Antonia in her silver, four-wheel-drive pickup. They met out past the oilfield-supply warehouses at the edge of town, beyond the paved road that ended at a ward of the Latter-Day Saints, at a site beside narrow dirt track. Antonia arrived first. She slowed near the surveyor's stake that would be their first position of the day, parked, and prepared field notes in the heated cab of her truck while Jet backed the drilling rig into place. Then Jet, who'd sharpened his work teeth testing bedrock for the failed Susitna Dam project in Alaska, stepped out into the ten-degree morning in full subzero field dress—overblown bunny boots, insulated coveralls, and black mesh *Torco Auger* cap under the hood of his fur-lined parka. Antonia didn't join him until he'd penetrated the ground to five feet. Then she tucked her headful of blonde curls under a hard hat with wool liner and emerged into the crisp, startling air.

Jet began each hole the same way. He raised the drilling

tower to vertical, an eager look on his face, until he'd aimed the diamond-bit tip at the slender, eighteen-inch-tall wooden stake. He fired up the diesel engine, which growled and complained as if new to this, and held the rig's round-handled lever in one gloved hand. Next he drained the last of a cold soda, belched mightily, and tossed the can into the nearest sagebrush. "Fire in the hole!" he yelled, as he cranked the sharp bit into soil. "Better get ready, geo! I'll have your first sample up in no time." He lit the third or fourth of the day's many cigarettes before turning his full attention to the changes in density with depth and the rate at which the auger spun.

They'd been on different schedules since before they met. Jet hadn't slept in two days before arriving in Utah: he'd flown nonstop from Anchorage, checked in at the company's Salt Lake headquarters, and declined to take a motel room there. "Too many temples in that town," he told Antonia later. He'd opted instead to drive the flatbed east up aspen-lined Parley's Canyon and continued south of the Uinta Mountains to Lavern. Meanwhile Antonia had preceded him from Salt Lake, through the snowy passes, eager to get started in her first real job since graduate school. *This is it!* she told herself—everything she'd worked for all her life.

After spending a day in site reconnaissance, she had checked in before dinner to the Dine-A-Ville Motel in Lavern. She expected the driller to do the same when he arrived that evening, but he headed straight for the town's only private club, the Cowboy Corral. He phoned Antonia hours later and in slurred words claimed he'd take the room next to hers when he was darn good and ready. She resolved to wait up to meet him but fell asleep before he arrived.

Waking at dawn, she'd been reassured by the sight of Jet's drill rig as big as a cement truck parked in the motel lot. Overnight, pockets of snow had collected around the tall tower, lowered for driving. On her way to breakfast, she peered into the cab. She was brought up short at the sight of three massive books on the front seat: *Utah Mining History, 1857 to Present. Volumes I - III*. Seeing the titles, her heart beat fast.

Onsite by nine in spite of his night out, Jet worked like two men as he brought samples up through the auger. Without speaking he handed them to Antonia. She in turn clamped them to the chain vise on the rig's flatbed and split them open. Though moist from first snows, the soil was still dry enough to crumble in her gloves. She wrote either "silty sand" or "sandy gravel" in her notebook, seeing a pattern in the layers: river deposits, thousands of years old. Ancient floodplain. Jet kept on through the subsurface, going deeper. Below the sand and gravel lay bedrock—hard as concrete and just as tough to pierce. When the auger struck it, Jet retrieved the drill tube, a dim-toothed smile on his face. Hitting rock near the surface meant it would bear pavement and they could stop. "*Finito*, geo," Jet said, every time. "There's another damn job shot in the ass."

Working in the brightening morning, she told herself she could stand the driller in country as open as this. Utah was wild and stripped to the bone. Strange and beautiful—rock exposed everywhere, naked and honest. The few trees were the size of mere shrubs, casting scant shadows, nothing like the deep, oak-filled woods back home. Even the colors of the earth were different here: hills of orange, spires of red, stripes of yellow in bald topography that stretched to every horizon. She hummed Puccini, *La Boheme*, which had once been her father's favorite opera. In the sunlight, among the many hues of rock, she was far from the hidden seams of coal and gray tailings of her youth.

Back in Salt Lake she'd asked her boss, "What's east of the Green River, Mr. Stevens?"

Dick Stevens hadn't looked up from his maps. He'd run one slender hand through his neat black hair. "Badlands, Castanero. Empty, useless desert."

Antonia had studied the site plan, her hands on her hips. "So . . . we're building a high-capacity road out there because . . . ?" It had to at least be a back route to the Colorado oilfields.

"Oh." Stevens squinted at her. "There's a ghost town out there. Called Bonanza. It was big on gilsonite extraction in the 1940s and 50s. Every old timer you talk to in the area, you'll find he worked in those mines."

"Old mining town?" Her face flushed.

"Yes. Long dead." He unfolded a color brochure. "Look at this." On the glossy cover, a photograph showed a vast rubber raft on a muddy river. Seated behind a dozen smiling people, an aging boatman held a pair of oars as long and thick as lightpoles. The caption read, "Colorado River Adventures, Cataract Canyon, Utah."

Stevens said, "Here's how we'll drill on the Green. We can load our rig right onto this outfit's biggest raft. They'll supply a veteran boatman to help." He looked up, meeting Antonia's silent apprehension. The skin around his gray eyes creased as he smiled. "You know how to swim, Antonia? The geologist before you didn't. He gave his notice when he saw this." Stevens waved the brochure and laughed, a thin intake of breath.

Blood warmed Antonia's face and hands. That they'd be working on water was news to her. Neither had she known about Bonanza and its mining roots. She kept her voice calm. "I can swim."

Before noon on the third day of drilling, just after shooting in the ass their fifth hole of the morning, Antonia and Jet wavered in their work. They couldn't find the next surveyor's stake and so had to walk the ground, searching. Antonia came upon it about fifty feet off the road, hidden in a mature ring of sagebrush. "Here it is." Stepping into the brush to read the label on the stake, she felt her feet crunch something brittle. She jumped back as if she'd been bit. "Bones!"

Jet came running. "Well, no shit." He tramped into the middle of them. A jumbled pile reached to his boot-tops: femurs, vertebrae, ribs—crisscrossed and heaped together, bleached white, picked clean and dry. He kicked aside a skull. "Coyote."

"All of them?"

"Looks like."

"What about those big skulls? Next to the three tiny ones right there."

"A whole family," Jet said, lighting a cigarette. "Somebody did good work here. Killed the little bastards before they could grow up and multiply." He smiled and exhaled smoke. "Saves the government from having to do it. Shit, maybe it was the government—clearing the way for our road."

"But, out here? Why not just . . ."

He looked amused. "Spit it out, geo."

" . . . let them escape." Her voice was small.

Jet had already turned toward a rumbling out on Asphalt Ridge. "Something's coming," he said. "Real slow."

"It sounds like a truck."

"Brilliant, geo. A damn big truck."

Antonia glared at him.

"Maybe it's the boatman," said Jet, checking his watch. "If so, he's right on time. Hell, I didn't know boatmen could read a clock."

A yellow truck twice the size of Jet's drill rig came into view. It had stake sides and an aluminum fishing boat turned belly-up atop its load. Grinding down the ridge, the driver was singing loud and out of tune to an old Willie Nelson song. The cacophony blasted from the cab's open window. The driver continued toward them until he slowed to a stop behind Antonia's truck. Turning off the radio and engine, he eased from the cab.

Antonia tried not to stare. Mr. Stevens' "veteran boatman" was the same oarsman she had seen in the rafting brochure. He stood short and thick from top to bottom, with trimmed white muttonchops, Day-Glo orange hooded sweatshirt, and dirty, worn cap that read *CRA*.

"Greetings, Earthlings," said the grinning stranger. He shook Jet's hand, then bowed to Antonia. "Name's Bert. Are you the ones expecting a boat?"

That afternoon they labored until dark to rig the thirty-three-foot pontoon raft. Antonia, acting as crew chief for the job, used her truck's mobile phone to call in a crane from town to help with the heavy lifting. They pulled two gigantic rubber tubes off Bert's truck, inflated them, and dragged them into place to form a sort of catamaran. Over the top of the rubber they slid a metal frame and tugged it into position. It came together inch by inch, like blowing up an enormous balloon. Through it all they spoke fewer than a dozen words an hour.

After the crane left, as Jet worked solo tightening down bolts on the now-floating drill rig, Antonia showed Bert the pile of coyote bones. He pulled a shovel from his truck without speaking and got to work burying them. He didn't comment until he'd finished, and then it was brief: "Assholes used poison—or traps."

That night Antonia phoned in an update to Dick Stevens. She caught him at home, the sound of soft music in the background. "We got the raft rigged, Mr. Stevens. We'll start drilling the river holes in the morning."

"Excellent, Castanero. How's it look?"

"It might work. If the Green doesn't rise."

"It won't. There shouldn't be snowmelt until spring."

Antonia held her tongue. She'd learned all too well about ice, rivers, and mid-winter warm spells from her father. But her boss wouldn't want to hear that story.

Stevens asked, "What's your take on the boatman?"

"A good guy and a hard worker."

"Great. Let him know he can stay on as Drilling Assistant. How is it out there?"

Antonia didn't mention her growing dread of the river job. Ice lay in the shadow of the streambanks. More ice would be coming in sheets: she'd heard that in winter the river filled with floes you could just about walk on. More and more the scene resembled the Susquehanna River, with its winter freeze-ups and fickle nature. She said nothing about her fears and nothing about the temperatures that were, in one of the driller's choice phrases, "butt-ass cold."

To Stevens, she said only, "There's excellent exposure. Everything's above ground—or close to it. Not much need for digging or stripping."

"Yes. Well." He coughed. "Good luck tomorrow."

Riding with Bert to the rig in the aluminum fishing boat each morning eased Antonia's dread of the river. He plied the many currents with obvious skill, even as rafts of ice dithered on the water's surface. The floes didn't melt, and he didn't waver. He just dodged them as if born to it, and he talked about the river with respect. "She's feeling cold this morning," Bert would say. "Got to be extra specially nice to her today."

"Papa used to talk like that," she said, "about the coal mine

101

in Port Griffith."

Jet worked on, all the while smoking, bossing Bert, and tossing profanity like stones. One morning he cracked a drill bit trying to pierce a boulder—"harder than shit, but way too shallow to be bedrock"—and headed back to town to buy a replacement. Bert and Antonia waited for him on the rig. She wasn't convinced Jet would get past the Cowboy Corral and be back before dark, but she didn't complain. Without the drilling jarring the raft, it settled down on the river and relaxed in its tethers from both shores. She sat cross-legged on the deck and turned her attention to her notes. Bert sat nearby, quiet a long time until out of nowhere he asked, "What got a girl like you interested in rocks?"

She looked up. "What do you mean, 'a girl like me'?"

Bert wore a serious expression. His cap, however, detracted from his gravity: Jet had stuck a piece of duct tape behind the "A" and marked it in felt pen with a tiny "p." Bert wore the "CRAp" hat with nonchalance—as if he knew it'd been altered but could've cared less. He raised his hands. "No offense. I just don't know any scientists, much less female ones."

"Geology is in my blood. My family's been in mining since the 1920s."

"No kidding? You ever work for the coal companies south of here?"

"No. I could never have anything to do with coal."

"Right." Bert nodded. A moment passed before he asked, "Why not?"

"I promised my father I wouldn't."

Antonia started her tale at the beginning. Her Grandpapa Castanero had grown up in the foothills of the Apennines. He'd begun in the coal mines at age thirteen, more than a decade before immigrating to Port Griffith, Pennsylvania, during the time of Mussolini. Antonia's father and three uncles had also dug coal since they were teenagers. They'd worked the River Slope Mine in Port Griffith long before Antonia was born. When she emerged from the womb in that coal-slag town, it was with a curiosity already intact about rocks. She grew to blacken her hands and clothes every day with the specimens she tossed and kicked apart. "Look at Tonia." Antonia's mother would point to the soiled fabric that became more and more difficult to clean. "Always filthy. I can't keep her out of the tailings."

Antonia's father, Francesco, only shrugged, the way he did at most things. "Let her be, Flo. She's got a brain, that Tonia. It'll get her out of this one-job town." Then he'd wander away as Flo wept silent tears. Antonia only learned later that her mother missed the happy Francesco that had wed her as a teen bride. Then, he'd never been without Musetta's waltz from *La Boheme*. He'd hummed it every morning: when he rose, when he shaved, when he left the house to meet his three brothers on their way to the River Slope, Puccini's aria had stayed with him.

Antonia told Bert, "I'm named for my Uncle Tony. He put money away for years to travel back to Italy, but instead his life savings sent me to college."

"Life savings? He's passed on?"

"Yes. Same with Uncle Joe. They died long before I was born." Antonia went back to her notes.

"I'm sorry." Many moments passed, filled only with the gossip of the river, until Bert whispered, "Antonia, look!" He pointed to the east bank.

She raised her binoculars. Peering across water the color of green olives, she searched the shore. First she saw just bare bank and leafless cottonwoods. The river glistened between the raft and land as she locked directly onto an animal sneaking a drink. "Coyote!" Antonia studied the golden-eyed gaze and sun-tipped fur.

"Dang," said Bert, "he'd better be careful. He's like Bambi at an NRA meeting out here."

"Worse. There's nowhere to hide."

"Yeah. Bambi at the South Pole NRA."

Antonia laughed but stopped when she remembered the pile of bones Bert had buried and the many sizes of skulls. Families, killed together—maybe even poisoned underground. And that bastard Jet, saying it was a good thing.

As if on cue, the driller drove into view over Asphalt Ridge.

Antonia let her binoculars fall on the strap around her neck. "Scram!" she cried. The coyote stared at the drill rig as if stunned it should speak. "Get out of here!"

The animal wheeled to a trot downstream.

The river work took a week. On land, drilling eight holes was a one-day job; on water, wet sands from the streambed flowed up into the auger. They jammed the bit before Jet could get to bedrock. Then the driller had to start the hole fresh, which he loathed and met with creative cursing. "Flowing sands," he said. "Always a bitch kitty." As the driller threw fits, he jolted the raft and rattled Antonia, and she did her best to ignore him. She focused on her notes and sketches of the subsurface she'd come to know from the samples—beds of unconsolidated sand and silt, occasional boulders, massive layers of sandstone.

Jet made it clear he couldn't wait to finish the eighth hole. "Damn this wet work." His drilling suit was coated with mud below the knees, his face and hair were splattered with fine brown droplets, and his knuckles were pitted with wounds from the times he'd had to work without gloves. His face had gone more gray with the cold.

Still, Jet persisted in the eighth hole until they hit bedrock.

When he pulled up the auger one last time, Bert prompted, "Another dang job . . . ?"

Jet stayed grim and didn't bite. When he did speak, he snarled the words. "Suit your damn selves, you two. I'm headed to town."

Bert said, "I'll go." He helped Jet stack the sections of auger as they were withdrawn from the earth.

Antonia agreed to join them in the Cowboy Corral once they'd all disassembled the raft. It came apart in a fraction of the time it had gone together. "Nice work, Castanero," Stevens said when she called him later from the Dine-A-Ville. "Ready for solid ground?"

"Yes, sir. We'll start again in the morning. Jet and Bert have punched out for the day."

"Understand. By the way, have the driller call me at home. I've got good news."

Antonia felt a red flag fly up but said, "Okay," and signed off. She headed for the Cowboy Corral to meet her drilling team. Fifteen minutes later she sat with Jet at the club as he sucked down beer after beer. She'd told him to call Stevens, and Jet had gone looking for a pay phone, returning in minutes with his eyes glittering. Bert had never even settled, instead prowling the tables for a dancing partner. He found one after two had said no and was now leading a jeans-clad redhead in a happy, floor-hogging Western swing. Eddie Rabbit played on the jukebox; the room was crowded and raucous. Antonia felt relief take hold in her.

She reached across the table for the pitcher near Jet. "Mind if I share that?"

"Suit yourself." He lifted his own beer and sucked it down greedily. His hair straggled below his plaid collar as he drained his glass. Forcing out a massive belch, he leveled a look at her. "So Monday it's just you and me again." Bert was headed home to Salt Lake with all his gear.

"Yeah. Too bad Bert's leaving. But we won't need him east of the river."

Jet poured himself another glassful. His eyes narrowed. "Ever been over there?"

"No. But I know there are oilfields. And the ghost town of Bonanza."

"Ghost town? That's what you think?" He snorted and looked around, at the pool tables, the bar lined with drinkers, the dancers wheeling on the raised parquet floor. "You ought to get out more, geo. Bonanza's going to boom bigger than southeast-fucking-Texas. Stevens and his rich buddies are going to bring in coal from Carbon County. They'll light up that old ghost town brighter than New York City."

"Coal?"

"Yup." Jet paused to suckle his beer. "Stevens sold me shares in the Deseret Plant."

"What Deseret Plant?"

"Only the biggest-ass coal-burning thingie in the two states! Out by Bonanza. You didn't know?" He tapped his forehead. "Well, I do. It's all going to come back. Banks, whore houses, saloons, mini-malls—all because of coal."

Antonia wiped sweaty hands on her jeans. "No one told me."

He raised a finger. "Very hush-hush. Had to clear all the railroad right-of-ways first. You know, to move the coal. But Stevens just told me we're as clear as the pope's ass. Hee hee hee. Sweet baby bastard Jesus—it'll be great!" He chuckled, then laughed with his head back, then roared until tears gathered on his lashes.

Bert returned from dancing. His CRAp cap was off; he wiped his damp forehead with a bandanna. "She's a great dancer," he said, nodding across the room. "Too bad her husband had to break in." Bert settled at the table as Jet continued to weep with laughter.

"Antonia?" Bert replaced and adjusted his cap. "What in the name of Jehovah is going on?"

Later that night, after she'd waited long enough for the inebriated Jet to turn in, Antonia knocked at Bert's motel room. After a minute he opened the door a crack and peered sleepy eyed over the little gold safety chain. She asked him for help, "out by the river."

He stood a moment, thinking. "There's a storm brewing."

She shrugged.

"Okay. Give me five." He clicked the door shut.

On her way to warm up the silver pickup, Antonia stopped at Jet's drilling rig. Once again she peered in the window. There it was—the three-volume history of Utah mining. She gazed back at the line-up of doors at the Dine-A-Ville. Quiet as the Port Griffith graveyard. She tried the door handle on Jet's truck. Unlocked. Reaching inside, she picked up the books—one, two, three—closing the door behind her with a quiet click. As Bert emerged from his motel room, she crammed the fat books behind her pickup's bench seat.

In minutes, she and Bert were headed east on Interstate 40. As she drove, Antonia could feel his eyes on her. "Let's hear it," he said.

She sighed. "When Mr. Stevens hired me, he said it was to 'consult on the paving of thirty-five miles of back road between Lavern and Bonanza.'"

"Isn't that what we've been doing?"

"He never said anything about coal."

"What about it?"

"The whole road's about it. That's what Jet told me tonight."

"And you've sworn off the stuff. But why?"

Without a glance, Antonia passed the turnoff they usually took to the river. What to say? She'd never explained her promise to her father to anyone.

"Antonia?"

She swallowed. "It was the River Slope Mine Disaster. In 1959. Back home in Pennsylvania. You ever hear about it?"

"Not a peep."

"See, the mine was near the Susquehanna River—you know, they found anthracite under the river floodplain. High-grade coal. They weren't supposed to dig beneath the river itself, but they did, past the safety stop line."

"Bad idea?"

"Yeah. See, the coal under there was too good to pass up." Crossing a bridge far upstream of their raft-drilling site, she turned south. The truck headlights swept over acres of rabbitbrush and sage fenced with barbed wire. "My uncles and my father always split up during their work, two and two. Just in case, they said. And all four of them were strong men—boys, really, in their teens and early twenties. But Jesus. The river was rising—this was January—it went from like two feet to fifteen feet in three days. There were ice floes, followed by some freaky warm weather . . . and . . . "

Bert waited. "And?"

"The river flooded. It broke through to that undercut part of the mine, even though they'd checked the braces that morning. There was ice water, just pouring in, and eighty-two men down there. Including Papa and my uncles."

Bert whistled, low and long.

"Tony and Joe were in the crew right under the river. Papa and Augie tried to find them but . . . they had to run the other

108

way. The water was three feet high and rising. Augie said it was like pushing through ice slush. It was up to their necks before he and Papa got roped out."

"And . . . the others?"

Antonia shook her head.

"God."

"Yeah." She told Bert the rest of the story: Uncle Augie was never able to hold a job long after that, Papa worked in the new vineyards and didn't make music any more—no humming in the morning, no Puccini, nothing. "And I studied rocks with Uncle Tony's money. On Papa's condition I never work for the mines. Bachelor's and master's in geology, Pennsylvania State University, magna cum laude."

Continuing onto open range, she slowed to allow a flock of sheep to clear the road. The route split and curved into limbs of a maze. At each fork, Bert consulted a topographic map, pointing which way to go. When they arrived at a chainlink fence surrounding a sign the size of Antonia's truck, she knew Jet had told the truth. Block letters printed in red and black on white read:

FUTURE SITE

BONANZA UNIT 1

Deseret Generation and Transmission

"Well, I'll be sheep-dipped," said Bert.

"Me, too." Antonia slowed nearly to a stop, taking in the words and bright insult of the sign in otherwise open, unspoiled country.

They continued west along good, paved road to Bonanza. In the moonlight the few remaining buildings looked whitewashed and new. Antonia found the end of the pavement and kept going on dirt road. When they reached the east side of the river, they stopped near shore. The water plodded by with no indication of their having labored day after day on it. The moon now hid behind clouds; the first flakes of snow drifted through the dark. Antonia couldn't see across the river to the tire tracks where they'd derigged the pontoon raft before going to town.

The stakes where Antonia and Jet were supposed to resume work led back toward Bonanza. They were positioned fifty feet apart, widespread like picket fenceposts.

"Now what?" asked Bert. His cap was off and his forehead lined with deep furrows.

"I don't know." Antonia slid the gear knob to neutral, pocketed her gloves, and stepped out into the night. With an ache she'd felt since the Cowboy Corral, she wandered through the desert scrub. She came upon a stake and kicked it. When it didn't budge, she put on her gloves to yank it up. Snowfall had become steady—still flaky, though, like ash from a distant fire. She continued along the road, knocking over another couple of stakes, collecting them. Bert followed in the pickup.

After several minutes he pulled up beside her and rolled down the passenger side window. "You'd better get in, Antonia. The snow's getting thicker. This is going to be a big one."

She nodded but kept walking. She came to a fourth stake at the top of a rise, wiping away tears. "Papa," she said. She removed the stake and stumbled. First light was still hours off, and the road was silent. The chill of the night urged her to join Bert in the heated cab. She tossed the four damp stakes in and climbed up beside them. Bert drove with Bob Wills singing low on the radio as they followed the dirt roads back through the badlands. A thin cover of white hid the tracks of the sheep they'd paused for earlier. In the middle of the Interstate bridge, Antonia said, "Stop, Bert. I want to get out here."

"No. Too cold."

She opened the door while they were still moving. Freezing air rushed in as she unsnapped her seatbelt.

"Criminey, Antonia!" Bert stopped.

She stepped out and to the bridge railing. She stood watching the river as he set the footbrake and hustled to her side. He took her arm. Chunks of ice careened into sight from under the bridge. With a jerk she pulled away from him.

"Don't!" He seized her shoulder.

"It's okay," she said. "I won't jump." Bert relaxed his grip, and Antonia returned to the pickup. She pulled the mining volumes from behind the bench seat. They were as heavy as telephone books.

Bert watched, eyes wide. "Aren't those Jet's?"

She nodded. "A little light reading. No, dark. Black, even." She stood at the bridge railing, now again with Bert's hand tight on her shoulder. She tossed the books off the edge, one two three. They splashed into the water and slipped below the surface. As an afterthought, she gathered the stakes from the truck and threw them into the river, too. They swirled away on the water like toy boats.

"That's it, Bert. Another damn job shot in the ass."

The high, chaotic song of coyotes pierced the night. Bert gasped, then threw back his head and roared. "A pack! Perfect timing."

She laughed, unbelieving at first, then full of joy, until tears came and streamed so fast there was no point in wiping them away.

They drove back the way they'd come, following pavement away from the site of the biggest-ass coal-burning thingie in two states. The snow fell thicker now. It was blown at an angle by a north wind, urged into the wipers Bert had switched on high. Antonia knew the way back, though no trace showed of their earlier tire marks; there'd be no trace of their new marks, either, by the end of the hour. She wouldn't come back out with Jet, she knew—if there was to be drilling at the remaining stakes, it would have to be without her.

Bert drove at a slow pace, talking low about the Colorado River many miles south: how deep into the earth it cut, how clear the sky was overhead. She'd have to go there, he said: she could be a geo-guide. It was safe on the river when you knew what to do. It sounded good to her; it sounded possible. In the glow of the headlights, Antonia saw the way before her grow more and more light.

Marooned

We arrive late and stand at the back of the crowd.

"Can you hear what they're saying?" I ask.

Mare shakes her head. "Not really. She said something about contributing to his enlightenment."

"Uh oh."

Mare giggles, then sighs as two-year-old Sammy squirms in her arms and fights his way to the ground. She follows as he wanders a crooked course toward the house and buffet tables. I'm left alone to watch the end of the ceremony over the dozens of heads before me.

The bride and groom, friends of Mare but strangers to me, have the American River canyon at their backs. Spring-green grass reaches nearly to their knees. He wears a slate-gray tuxedo with creamy white boutonniere. She is big eyed in a long dress and wide-brimmed straw hat, her train draped over one arm.

The afternoon breeze bends toward me, carrying the distant scream of a red-tailed hawk. Mare has said this place brings back memories of working on the river: days guiding tourists through whitewater, camping on sun-warmed beaches, sleeping at the water's edge. The breeze bends again and bears the final words of the wedding: "You may kiss." The bride and groom share a long kiss as the river's rush rises from hundreds of feet below, filling a hush that precedes the inevitable wave of laughter from the guests. The groom raises a triumphant fist. His bride smiles, all radiance and indulgence, and strolls arm in arm with him to the champagne table for their first toast.

Mare and Sammy return. "I remember repeating those same words," I say. "'I do' and 'I will.'"

"I know, Sue." Mare's face draws in sympathy.

"Maybe it will work for them."

"It may still work for you."

"No way I'd take Tom back now."

"But you might. It's not over until the fat lady sings."

"Show me where she is. We'll harmonize."

The crowd is not supposed to dig into the food until three o'clock, but guests are edging close to the *hors d'oeuvres*. After the first hand plucks up a California roll, it's all over, and a scramble begins for foam plates and plastic forks. It's a pot-luck wedding, but not everyone has brought a dish, and there's a bit of a shortage. Polite panic builds. I weave my way in and manage to heap a plate with potato salad, mesquite-grilled salmon and halibut, French bread, and foil-wrapped squares of butter. With my fingertips I grab two forks and two bottles of lime sparkling water and settle on the redwood deck.

Mare and Sammy share my plate as the groom and his best man link arms to dance on the lawn. The two men lip-sync to the Rolling Stones, who wail *in absentia* from stereo speakers perched in open windows above the deck. The best man's hair swings in a ponytail past his shoulder blades, brushing the back of his matching tuxedo. The guests chuckle and applaud.

"They do dance well together," says Mare.

"Amazing. Do you think they rehearsed it?"

The first champagne cork flies over the lawn and into long grass as the music segues to a solo guitar arrangement of Tchaikovsky's "Sleeping Beauty Waltz." The happy couple clasp hands to begin their first dance, their faces confident, their eyes meeting.

"Now that looks rehearsed," says Mare.

"Yeah. Mine was, too."

Mare nods, her eyes sympathetic, then turns to her son. "Hey, Sammy, you know this song—'Once Upon A Dream.'" They sing together, the boy eager and joyful, his mother bending to hold him. Moments later, Sammy focuses on my empty water bottle and the serious art of depositing pine needles in it.

"Oh, Mare, he's great."

She nods. "Most of the time."

"Tom didn't want kids."

Mare reaches an arm around me. "It's okay. You'll have a family, Sue. Even Jack took some convincing."

"It's too late now."

"With Tom, maybe."

The wedding party is dancing on the lawn. Arms wave, champagne spills, tuxedo tails whip and fly. Ecstatic couples jump and sing to an upbeat rhythm and blues.

As the best man prances, eyes closed, a sheath-wrapped blonde partner joins him. Their hips meet, neat and narrow, as they bounce to the music. Dirty dancing. I watch their gleeful faces until I cannot breathe. "Mare, I have to go."

"I'm sorry. This wasn't a good idea. Here, we'll walk you to your car."

Purple brodaiea and wild iris line the dirt road that descends from the wedding to the river. The road clings to steep hillside. A wire fence and faded posts provide the thinnest barrier between the shoulder and a precipitous reach of canyon. I could swerve toward the edge and pull three strands of barbed wire with me as I plummet over the cliff, airborne for just seconds before the first great bounce. Maybe the car would roll a half dozen times before falling, perhaps even in flames, to the river. The sheriff's team would spend days recovering my charred remains, no longer recognizable even to my remorseful husband.

But I don't swerve. I take my time, attentive to the lupine and poppies and clusters of wild onion upslope. The road levels off near the river, where the forest's fragrance drifts in my open window. Live oak and digger pine arch the road. The sound of rapids grows louder, and I pull over.

Something's wrong. Crowds have gathered at the river's edge. Mid-stream in heavy whitewater, a rubber raft is plastered on a huge rock. Four wet boaters huddle on the big boulder, clinging to the deflated and sorry-looking raft. Clearly, their guide is not with them. On the opposite bank, a group of spectators point cameras, wave, and shout. Guides from other rafts have pulled to shore and now rush on paths through the willows to help. I leave my car, as drawn as the others by the gravity of the scene: novices stranded on a wrapped boat in a cold river.

A young, dark-haired guide stands poised on land, watching the foaming water. She must be the missing guide; she must have fallen out mid-run. She can't be more than nineteen years old. Strapped to her lifejacket is a diving knife. Arms crossed, in all stillness, she studies the currents. Her deliberation courses with electricity. With a great rush and lift of arms, she plunges and swims, head down, angled into the stream, to reach the rock.

"Right," I say.

Her arms churn, her legs kick. The eyes of the shipwrecked

paddlers are on her, their shoulders sagging as she washes downstream past them. As the river carries her away, it seems there's no hope, but she keeps stroking, stroking, not giving up. Ultimately, her determination drives her forward, and she catches the tail end of the eddy. She rides the backwater to its splashing surge against the rock.

"So now what?" I ask. "Now you're marooned, too."

She clambers up to talk with her people. They shake their heads. She confers with them for many minutes during which none of them looks convinced. Nothing changes until finally they shrug and check the straps on their lifejackets. Together, the five step to the edge of the rock. Joining hands, they jump into the current and wash through the tail waves to the bottom of the rapids. In moments they have thrashed their separate ways to shore, where the dark-haired girl herds them up a boulder bar, away from danger.

"Of course," I say, convinced I never doubted her.

It's not until I have driven to the narrow bridge over the river that the tears come. They cover my face, and I let them, as I remember another dark-haired girl who tried and never stopped, who never gave up even when it seemed there was no hope. My hair is shorter and laced with silver now, but I'm still that same girl.

Parking near the Coloma Grange Hall, I walk back over the bridge. Mid-river, I lean over the downstream wall, my weight against old stone. A few leaves course on the water beneath me. They dip, rise, and are carried downriver.

The Wish

B Barton has water deep in his bones, but you can't tell it by looking. His face is leathered and creased with lines, and his arms are as tan as adobe up to his elbows where he rolls his shirtsleeves. I look at B and think sun, dust, and wind—desiccated before his time—and like me not much over thirty. Never in a million years did I suppose when he first came through the Oasis's double doors that he's connected to things wet. He's got the best spring in a hundred miles, and he knows groundwater the way most people know their names. Why he looks drier than the dirt roads leading here beats the hell out of me.

Maybe it's this place. Most parts are drier than lizard skin. Canyons reach from town in all directions, no streams in them—just rock and gravel, cleared out by heat and wind. Here and there around the backcountry you find wells and a couple of pretty green springs like the one B lay claim to. Any water you stumble on is more precious by far than the gemstones the average rockhound spends years seeking in the mountains.

Or maybe we're drawn to opposites, which would explain B's being here, as well as the presence of the rest of the misfits who come in search of a suitable geography. Or, as B says, "Not misfits, Sue—iconoclasts." None of us could have picked a more arid place to land, just thirty miles east over the Amargosas from Badwater and Death Valley. Outside the Oasis, our main street is as dry as those godforsaken pieces of earth.

Definitely an iconoclast, that B. Not an easy one to know. At first I saw him in here only a few times a month. When he did turn up, the rest of the guys would pause at the pool table and bar like they'd been expecting him. They'd all listen long enough to hear his jeep grind to a stop out in the lot. Soon B would push open both front doors, flooding the room with daylight. He'd stretch his neck like it hurt and settle in front of me at the bar. The others would go back to their drinks and pool shots.

"Evening, B," I would say.

"Good evening, Sue."

I'd set him up with three full glasses of water, no ice, followed by a mug of draft. He always hit the water first, lifting each glass in turn. When he brought the water to his lips, there was no gulping. No obvious chugging. He just slid the water in, as Fred the caretaker of the Herkimer Guest Ranch said, "like he was a quart low and about to burn the engine."

B's good looks throw you. He's got eyes so blue you'd think you were gazing through him to the sky. He has manners, too, which believe me out here is rare. When I took this job two years ago, he came in and asked in his polite way for the waters and beer. As I poured, he walked back out to his jeep and I thought, oh hell, he's gone, but he returned with a paper bag of crystals to show me—all amethyst, all sizes. He drew pictures on a handful of cocktail napkins: maps, arrows, scribbled words. He sketched wild canyons he'd found all around the desert where there were hidden gemstones. Standing across the bar from him, I lost my sense of east and west in deep, winding gorges. I could have drowned in his tales of palm oases below cliffs stark enough to be on the moon. All this beauty I'd never seen, edged with wind-rustling fronds of water-loving trees, all described by him.

One time B pulled out a small, perfect violet crystal. "This is my favorite. At first I thought it was just a big flake of mica." It had been a gleam in the sand along the Amargosa River, a shine in the dust he'd passed up at first. He'd dug down and glimpsed more, and he kept going, following the sparkle. When he lifted it out, he knew it was a well-formed amethyst with color as deep as lilacs. No bigger than my thumb, that crystal. It had unpitted faces that shined like the sky after a storm.

Months passed, and B took to spending more time at the Oasis. Often he promised he'd take me far up his canyon to see his spring. After too long of hearing that, I said, "You know, B, I'm starting to think you're full of it. All these beautiful places only you know about. This famous spring of yours where nobody goes."

He lifted his right eyebrow—a peeved look. "I'm going there tomorrow. I'll take you. We can meet here, right out front."

I told him I'd believe it when I saw him in the morning.

That evening I closed up the Oasis by myself. The last thing I did before going home was clean the bathroom in back. I washed the sink and mirror first, then the toilet. As I mopped my way out of the little room, I stopped to pull outdated announcements off the wall. Of course I didn't touch the timeless bumper stickers that would have been hell to peel off anyway. They said things like, "Women Want Me, Rocks Fear Me" and "I'm Retired—I Was Tired Yesterday and I'm Tired Again Today." There were business cards thumb-tacked up for everything from farriers to haircutters. Then there was the thing I always read last, a poem typed on a sheet of yellowed paper that I would never remove.

The Wish

Oh! To see blue waves
Roll mute upon the shore
Shells with all their secrets
Sweep back into the foam

Oh, if you and I
Met as sea meets sky
Suffused. Never ending
Blending, damp with fog

Those few words captured the coast where I grew up: the gray skies I didn't miss, the rain I did. I offered my usual prayer to the page and asked it for a sign I should stay in the desert. "Lonely as a fisherman in Death Valley," I said. Then I finished closing and went home.

In my trailer across the highway, I lay on my bunk listening to jazz: Wes Montgomery, Bill Evans, and Thelonious Monk on a CD mix I'd burned years before. Music washed through me. As the tunes drifted low, they eased me down; as they climbed high, they lifted me up. Soon I felt as light as a cork on water, and sleep carried me away.

B arrived at the Oasis at first light. I'd gotten ready to go, just in case. We drove east toward Tecopa Pass, no words between us. Rays of sun brightened the sky but hadn't yet hit ground. B had his jeep radio on but turned low, playing mostly the scratchy sound of static. The skinny dirt road, bent by the curve of the Earth, went all the way to the horizon. There were few crossroads to speak of. Hawks sat on telephone poles, watching the ground. Over it all—road, poles, hawks, mountains—the morning light flowed soft. It wasn't harsh, or rough. B took it all in with the familiarity of someone in his backyard.

Once we crossed Tecopa Pass, we entered another dry valley, staying on the graded road. According to B, we were climbing into the Kingston Range. Passing the sign and turnoff to the Underdog Mine, B and I glanced up the wide canyon. Two hard-working family men had been at their jobs up there for twenty years: Barry and Jerry, the only miners who ever brought their wives when they visited the Oasis. Fred from the Herkimer had said more than once that Barry and Jerry were "the best of the friggin' lot." They got plenty of talc from the Underdog, more than came from any other mine in the Kingstons. As I thought of Fred, we passed his spur road, marked only by a modest wooden arrow.

B drove on. After climbing a minute more, we pulled onto a track through scrub and scattered yucca. Back from the main road, B stopped to open a gate at the mouth of his canyon. We continued beyond the fence into a stand of willows and cottonwoods, not parking until we arrived at a tiny camp kitchen. My heart filled with joy when I saw the sedge-lined pool beside his stove and roll-up table. Maidenhair fern grew at the fringes; dragonflies as big as hummingbirds darted over the unruffled surface. A mockingbird whistled, then chattered, then warbled. Clear, inviting water flowed from a pipe, and B stuck his hand into the stream. His eyes glowed as he wet his fingers.

"All this water comes from your spring?" I asked.

He nodded and motioned toward the mountain. "Yeah. There's more farther up. We can go there sometime when it's not so hot."

Another bird called from across the pool. Its voice started low, climbed high, and then fell again. B frowned. "Quail. Hear that? Always singing my wife's name. 'Re-BEC-ca. Re-BEC-ca.'"

My heart dropped at the mention of a wife, but I said, "I'm

married, too. My husband was a logger in Fort Bragg."

"Ah." B pulled a dandelion from the edge of the pool. "You lived on the ocean."

"Yeah. The opposite of here."

"Rebecca was from Astoria, in Oregon."

Astoria and Fort Bragg had rain in common. Storms blew in off the sea, black and sudden. Tom and I used to hold each other in bed, listening to gales we thought would lift the roof. The wind and rain pinned us there, like ocean-going birds forced onto rocks along shore.

"Is she there now?"

"No. She's been dead five years."

"I'm sorry."

B studied me. "Where's your logger husband?"

"Las Vegas. At Harrah's, dealing blackjack. We're . . . separated." Tom's logging job had ended when the big trees got scarce. He moved to Vegas a few months ahead of me. By the time I'd sold our home in Fort Bragg to follow him, he'd been sharing his apartment with a stripper for three weeks. He couldn't resist all that skin, he said, after years of seeing women dressed only in wool plaid.

I shrugged. "I found the Oasis job in the penny paper and applied."

B looked thoughtful. He held a stone no bigger than a deck of cards. "Sue, do you know what this is?"

"A rock."

"What kind?"

"A gray one." I shrugged. "Marble?"

"No. It's much softer than that. Feel it, you can scratch it with your thumbnail." He put the smooth, flat rock in my hand.

My heart leapt at his touch. "This rock . . . feels greasy."

"Right. It's talc. A clay mineral—with water in its structure. You've heard of it, right? Soapstone? Rocks don't come much softer." He leaned close and whispered. "Its name comes from the Arabic. *Talk*. Means it's full of secrets. It only shares them when ... heated."

My blood pounded so hard I was sure he'd notice.

That evening B stayed for dinner at my fold-down table. He washed dishes and I dried as we listened to Sonny Rollins on the CD player. I swayed to the rhythm of the saxophone. When we'd finished cleaning up, I made a pot of decaf. B and I sat down with mugs Tom and I'd bought at the Tradewinds coffee shop in Fort Bragg.

"What's this music, Sue?"

"Old standards. Jazz. I never get tired of it."

"Jazz has always left me cold."

"No way."

"What do you like about it?"

"I don't know. I can't explain it."

"Try." He smiled the short distance across the table.

"Well. It takes its time, and I like that. There's the head— the melody—at the beginning. Then there's all the improvising. The players try on the song in every imaginable way. They just ... go off with it."

B nodded. "Go on."

I closed my eyes. "It doesn't travel a straight line. The music wanders, but it doesn't get lost. It explores, you know? Then it returns to the head, much ... " I stopped, feeling self conscious.

"Much?"

"Deeper. When it comes back to the head, it ... enters my veins, is all I can say. It drives in more than if it hadn't strayed. Like—the rewards are greater for all that searching. The sweetness is sweeter, or shininess shinier, like . . . "

"Like?"

"Like a gemstone." What I didn't say was, *like that perfect amethyst crystal you dug up on the Amargosa. After all those years of looking.* "And then I'm found. I'm back to where I started and at the same time farther along. I'm where I've been wanting—wishing—to be. And I feel lucky. Like I'm home."

I opened my eyes. A startled-looking B faced me. He got to his feet a bit at a time, stretching his neck like it pained him. *Oh, crap,* I thought, *he's leaving.* But no, he leaned across the table and kissed me. It was long and slow, turning over a warm feeling inside me.

Then he pulled back, his eyes wide like he'd forgotten something. "I'd better go." In a moment he'd pushed out the door of my trailer.

Don't go, I yearned after him. *Come back.*

B stayed clear of the Oasis for days after that. He didn't stop in once, not even to town as far as I knew, which after having kissed him put me in a state of mind. The other guys noticed, and they asked lame questions, like "Hey, Sue, where'd you hide the body?" and "Does this mean the wedding's off?" Real jerk-off material. When forty-eight hours passed and there was still no B, I called Fred to ask if he knew anything, if he'd seen B coming and going. He said no, but he'd check around. "He's hid out before," said Fred. "Since his wife died. But damn. It's been a while."

One night after work, I lay in the dark listening to Monk. B was on my mind even as the music played—through patterns of climbing scales and improv that went on and on. The flow of notes didn't transport me as usual, so I turned on the light. My mind wouldn't settle. A few minutes later, I heard scratching on my screen door. I sat up. "B?"

"No, Sue, it's Fred. Sorry. I never did know how to knock on these things."

"No problem, Fred. Come in."

"Can't stay. Been in Vegas and have to get back to the Herkimer." He stood outside with his hands in his overall pockets. "Has he showed?"

"No." I opened the door and stepped onto my wooden stairs.

"Figures. It's that damn spring of his. He's worked it like a slave since he lost Rebecca four—no, five—years ago."

"How'd she . . . pass on?"

He pushed back his cap. "It was the weirdest friggin' thing. She had that illness where you can't eat or drink—what's that called?" Fred looked away. "Oh, yeah. 'Failure to thrive.'"

"But only seniors and babies get that."

"No. Anybody can. She hated it here, couldn't stand things dry. Still . . . I mean, come on. No one thought she'd up and dehydrate herself to death. After that B worked around the clock to improve his spring. Planted new palms, rows of them. 'Where there are trees, there's water,' he told me. Damn. I always thought it was the other way around."

That figured. On the north coast, the creeks all but stopped flowing when the forests were cut. Once the logging robbed them of shade, entire watersheds went dry.

B transformed the Golden Rule claim. He built rock structures to deepen the pools and, in addition to palms, planted cottonwoods and willows to attract songbirds. He showed Fred how to restore the oasis at the Herkimer, too. "He helped me bring it back. Now I've got hummingbirds and dragonflies. Happy as larks. A ring of palm trees where bighorn sheep stop for shade. Shrubs with little red berries the guests go ape for. Hell, you've seen the place."

"It's the best around."

"Nope." Fred shook his head. "Compared to B's upper spring, the Herkimer's naked as a baby's butt. He's got so many birds you could be at the damn zoo. And wet. He's raised the water table back up. Like he's a friggin' magician—there's water so near the surface it fills your bootprints right behind you. B did all that."

"Not in time to save Rebecca."

"Maybe not. But she wasn't too tough. Fragile, even. Kind of an Emily Dickinson type, into poetry. As if . . . well, you've seen her writing. In the bathroom at the Oasis? A poem called 'Hoping' or 'Wishing' or—"

"'The Wish'?"

"That's it. She wrote that. B put it up there."

After Fred left, I kept picturing B out at his spring, working late into the night. And keeping his upper spring to himself. It pissed me off, him staying away like that. I dressed for a drive and headed for the washboarded road toward his claim. There was no moon. Other than my headlight beams and the dust blowing up red in my taillights, everything looked dark—the blackness of sky and mountains blending together.

Light shone from the pass, in the direction of B's canyon and spring. Some of the ridges were lit up like the sun was still out. As I drove closer, I saw it wasn't B's claim shining like a million diamonds. It was the Underdog, Barry and Jerry's talc mine.

When I stopped and stepped out of my pickup, I heard the ringing of metal against metal, then silence for a minute, then the grinding of a power saw blade, followed by more metallic ringing. I couldn't see much, just an eerie glow cast onto the rock walls. The noise came and went, stopping now and then before starting up again with more fury.

After many minutes, I saw someone coming from up the road, first obvious only as a pair of khaki pants, then as a white shirt above them, growing bigger. It had to be B, lit up by the radiance from the canyon. When he came near, I saw his smile, his teeth gleaming bright in his tan face. I was about to ask where in hell he'd been all these days, but the cacophony started again at the talc mine.

I yelled, "B, what in God's name is going on up here?"

"Beats me! It's like Dante's inferno!"

He pulled a small flashlight from his hip pocket but kept the beam off as he waved me to follow him across the road. We moved like two cats, B first and me behind him imitating his stealth walk. As we passed the Underdog's base camp, I couldn't help but feel underwhelmed by the bare-bones outdoor kitchen with its canned food, dishes drying on a card table, and row of beat-up five-gallon jugs for their water supply.

During a break in the noise, I whispered, "*This* is 'the best of the lot'?"

"Shh. If they find us here they might get nasty."

"Right, B. Barry and Jerry nasty?"

"I'm serious. That emergency clinic in town is there for a reason. Plenty of miner's heads have been busted over places like this."

We pushed through the willows and rushes. Where the plants ended, we stopped at a dark, damp spot on the ground. B lit it with his flashlight. "I thought so," he said.

"What?"

"They must've blasted the mother rock all to hell. Look at this sorry piece of guano. It used to be the twin sister to my oasis, but I'm guessing it drained out through the fissures they made with their dynamite."

My heart fell a couple of feet. I wanted to reach my hand out to B. Instead I could only follow him up the canyon as he took off again, now lighting our way through the ocotillo and cholla. After a minute of my trailing him, we edged together onto a rock ledge where we could look down on Barry and Jerry. They were a hundred feet below wearing goggles and hardhats and sweating over their work in the cool night air. They bent over a huge wooden workbench that looked as unmovable as bedrock. A generator ran klieg lights that flooded the place with eye-stunning brightness. Between the mighty hammer swings that crashed metal on metal, the tiny sound of their boombox broke through the din. I knew the music, though I no longer listened to that genre: Led Zeppelin, from the *Hindenburg* album.

We watched only a few minutes before B signaled we should leave. I followed him again, through the skeletal desert flora, then along the road to my truck. He leaned in, and I thought he'd kiss me, but he didn't. He turned to go.

"I know about Rebecca!" I said.

He wheeled back to me, his eyes flashing in the glow from the canyon.

I swallowed. "I just want to say it's okay."

"Okay?"

"Fred told me the desert killed your wife."

B's mouth fell open. "That's what people think?"

"I love 'The Wish.'"

He snorted. "It failed."

"What? To bring water? To . . . ?"

He shot me an angry look, and in a second he was gone. His white-shirted figure grew smaller and more dim, then went to nothing, as he jogged up the road to the Golden Rule.

Crap. There wasn't anything to do but retreat the other way, into the darkness I'd come through earlier.

When I reached my trailer, I put Monk on the CD player. I listened, wondering what to do. Call Fred to tell him B was all right—if you could call it that? No. Fred, like most normal people at two a.m., would be sound asleep.

Days later B knocked on my trailer door so early the sun hadn't yet hit the tips of the Amargosas. He stood on my front step, his work clothes coated with silt. A bruise colored his chin and cheek, and he held a red bandanna to his face. When he lifted the cloth, I saw one of his eyes was swollen shut.

"God, B! What happened?"

He waved me off. "We've got to get going."

"Where?"

"We can talk on the way."

First I packed ice from my freezer into a plastic bag. "Not without this."

We started off in the pre-dawn air, with his jeep's soft top rolled up and me at the wheel. B iced his face as I drove and snuck looks at him. "Did Barry and Jerry work you over?"

He groaned from the pain. "No. I stepped on the rake I use to clean out my pool. The wooden handle flew up and hit me in the face. Hard."

"Oh, good one. 'Man Attacked by Garden Tool.'"

He grinned, then winced. "Ow. Don't make me laugh."

We rolled up to the one stop sign in town on Highway 127. Turning left would lead us to B's spring. Turning right would take us to Badwater, out in Death Valley.

"Go right," he said.

I cranked the wheel. The road to Badwater stretched out

before us. The rearview mirror was full of the sunlight that would soon burst over the Kingstons.

After a few miles, B said, "I'm such an idiot."

"How so?"

"Barry and Jerry did come looking for me." He moved the ice pack. "And that thing they were building? A tub for water. A beautiful object. They'd meant to make it for Rebecca years ago. It's even engraved."

"Engraved?"

"Yeah. With two words."

"Let me guess. 'Golden Rule.'"

"No," he said. "No. It says, 'The Wish.'"

Tears wet my cheeks. B didn't notice, I don't think, with that icepack still on his face. We kept on, arriving at the salt flats near Badwater just as the sun broke above the horizon. Light hit the tops of the Panamint Mountains to the west. Their peaks blushed pink. More light flowed into the valley, the warmth of the sun taking the edge off the night's chill. On the flats a web of mudcracks reached from the edge of the parking lot where we stood.

B's swollen face had gone down a little. He shaded his eyes as the mud came into the sun. Then we heard it: a single, small pop. Silence followed, then a snap, sudden like a snare rim shot, random like popping corn.

I turned to B, my eyes wide.

He looked happy. He put his arms around me and stood close. His heart beat against my ribs. "It's the salt crystals. They break as the mud warms and expands. It means there's water in the layers. Talking to us."

"Singing to us."

When the sun came full on the flats, the mudcrack choir

went wild. It didn't last long, slowing to one pop every ten seconds, then one every half minute, then less. When it stopped altogether, I faced B for a long embrace. Soon we stood apart, then made our way back to the jeep, where we rolled down the top. With me driving again, B spilled actual tears.

"Okay," was all he said. He kept weeping, and I just let him, figuring he'd have to let it out. He'd have to let it flow. There was nothing to do but hold the wheel and think of the music as we followed the highway home.

An Exposition of the Development of the Earth

Near the end of his life, my maternal grandfather pulled me into the middle of his story. "Thank you for beginning your new book *in media res*, Mare," he wrote. As always, his penciled cursive slanted to the right; it almost floated off the page, so light was his hand. "In *Dryland* (superb title), I'm hooked from the first scene. *Brava!*" Using perfect grammar and complete sentences, he detailed his admiration for my second environmental crime novel ("outdoor murder mystery," he called it). His letter outlined evidence of his close reading. Then, after three chatty pages, he asked, "something near to my heart. I'm finishing a scientific treatise on the formation of the Earth. Can you help me complete it?"

I telephoned my mother Joan, B.S. Stanford, M.S. Princeton, Ph.D. Berkeley, professor of Earth Sciences at UCLA, and my grandfather's only child. She had just a minute to talk. She sighed, an exhalation no doubt forcing out the ubiquitous cloud from a cigarette. "You'd smoke, too, if you lived in L.A.," she once told me. "It's recreational, Mare. Like your river trips."

I brought up Grandpa's request. "Have you read his work?"

"Glanced at it. He theorizes an accelerating Earth. Quite unique."

"He says he needs help."

"Well, at age eighty-five . . ." Perhaps she was looking out her window then, thinking of her father's growing frailty. Time had whittled him down so his shirts appeared bigger every year. "Wish I could lend a hand, but my course load already keeps me in irons. Besides." She laughed. "You know how wary he is of institutions. To him, I'm one of the 'educated idiots.' You, on the other hand, being both a boater and published author, are held in high esteem. Oh God! Look at the time. Mare, hon, I've got to go teach."

Saying goodbye to the already silent line, I hung up and dialed Grandpa's number. If I called through the time zones any later, he and Grandma would be watching *M.A.S.H.* reruns, which they'd never abandon for a ringing phone.

Grandma picked up, her voice quavering as it had for years. "Al's in the barn loft. Hang on, I'll get him." She set down the handset with a light tap. I envisioned her hurrying to the back door to find her husband of five decades, her customary cardigan thrown over bony shoulders. I checked my watch once, then again. I was due to pick up my son Sammy at school.

"Hi, girl." Grandpa answered minutes later, his breath labored. "Sorry to keep you waiting. There's no fast way down that ladder."

He queued up his question with care, as if building a long-needed bridge. In his opinion, scientists hadn't "adequately described the mechanism" to explain the presence of similar fossils on separate continents. "And my work does. I just need help completing it—and publishing it. That's where you come in, Mare."

"Grandpa, I'm no scientist. I write novels—I spin them out of thin air."

"Exactly!" His slight lisp grew stronger. "You have a keen sense of story. That's critical to good science writing. I'm thinking of the sources you must have used for *Extinction*. Very convincing."

My cheeks filled with blood. My grandfather didn't know how much I'd pulled my first novel from imagination.

"Besides," he said, "you have another equally important qualification."

"Which is?"

"You're published. You know what it takes to get into print. We'd be co-authors."

"Do you have a journal in mind?"

"*S_____ Magazine*, of course. Top of the line for work like this. And Mare, in case you need incentive, your mother said you'd like to have my guideboat. Help me with this, and it's yours."

"Blackmail! Grandpa, I hate to rush, but I have to get Sammy at school. Send me your paper, okay? I'll take a look."

"Thanks, girl." His voice sounded both fierce and fragile. "You're a good one."

Replacing the receiver, I stared at it a moment before running out the door, car keys in hand.

My grandfather's guideboat was the only thing of his I coveted. I'd admired it since my teens, when I'd learned to pull a pair of oars: it was as narrow as a canoe, braced inside with curved ribs, and fitted like a dory with brass oarlocks. Guideboats had been the craft of choice in upstate New York in the first half of the twentieth century, after which the boats had dwindled in number. They were rare anywhere, but especially out West—all the more reason I wanted to drive one home to Utah someday.

This particular guideboat was a bit of an anomaly. Built by Fred Rice, it was found wrecked and abandoned on a lake in the Adirondacks where my grandfather worked as a summer guide. "Rice was the best craftsman," said Grandpa. "Everyone wanted his boats." Being a skilled woodworker himself, and a man who'd fished from everything that floats, Grandpa rebuilt the guideboat using home-milled wood and fiberglass. The synthetic material might have raised eyebrows in the purists' circle, but I didn't question it. If he believed a hull needed resin and glass, it did. Through the years he used the boat most weekends, exploring little strings of lakes and escaping to the quiet of fishing.

He'd never before raised the subject of who should inherit the guideboat when the time came. Joan and I had described it to specialists at the Adirondack Museum during a visit, thinking a Rice boat belonged there, but they doubted the historical value of a boat patched with fiberglass. Until the phone call about his manuscript, I'd never considered I might bring Grandpa's legacy West.

Since his eyes had clouded at age seventy, he'd relied on others to row him, resigning himself to passenger status. I'd been the latest guest at his oars, having flown to Rochester alone while my husband Jack stayed home with Sammy. I drove south to Geneseo through a golden autumn, following the hushed river. As always I calmed with every mile of distance from the airport. Pulling into my grandparents' neighborhood, I took solace in the piles of yellow and orange leaves on the lawns and the unfenced backyards with gardens bearing the season's last vegetables. Inside my grandparents' two-story former farmhouse, stale smoke lingered from their decades-old cigarette habits. In the upstairs bedroom that had been theirs in earlier years, I opened a window to let in fresh air.

Next morning Grandpa and I launched the guideboat on a farm reservoir outside town. He sat on the bow seat, facing me with outstretched legs. The double-ended hull glided through the water as if new. Grandpa searched shore, his eyes perhaps taking in the colors of the changing woods but not distinguishing species of tree as they once had.

"My eyesight's really shot," he said. "I wonder what ability I'll lose next." Sunlight filtered through a fall haze. I rowed the lake's perimeter, smelling the sweetness of decaying leaves. A loon called across the water. "Hear that?" Grandpa put a hand behind one of his enormous ears. "Migrant. Passes through every year. Used to be little flocks of them, but now we just get one or two." We listened for more. Silence.

After a minute, he said, "Tell me how you learned about species loss."

I shook my head. "I know hardly anything."

"But in *Extinction*, your protagonist considers taking her own life when the Ivory-Billed Woodpecker is presumed gone. What inspired that?" He scanned the shoreline, as if he could make out detail.

"Just a hunch. It's an urge I get myself when a species winks out."

He swung his gaze toward me, his foggy eyes wide.

"Don't worry." I forced a grin. "I won't act on it."

He didn't smile. "We have to persevere constantly, Mare. We have to—" The loon called again. "There! Like the loon. We have to stick with it year after year."

My head throbbed, growing achy. I closed my eyes, still rowing, until Grandpa warned me I was off course. Readjusting for another time around the smooth lake, I felt my face flush with embarrassment.

Back near my grandfather's Chevy Impala, we disembarked, gripped the gunnels of the boat, and swung it to the roof racks. My head pounded as I bore most of the weight of the lifting.

Still, it was Grandpa who groaned and bent forward in pain. He couldn't hide his pale face and set lips as he waved off my concern. "It comes and goes."

We drove back to town through rolling drumlin valleys dotted with old farms and scattered new homes. Grandpa's presence beside me felt transient in a way it never had all the summers I'd spent with him and Grandma—he was thinner, ghost like.

In a slight voice, he said, "You're a good driver, Mare. An accomplished oarswoman, too. I think you're ready for that boat."

I didn't respond. If I spoke, I'd want to tell him something he might find sentimental: that I craved the boat now because it carried the light of a fall day and the memory of him riding in the bow.

Grandpa's manuscript arrived on a Friday afternoon in November. My family and I were preparing for a weekend away—Sammy and Jack packing a bag of plastic trucks while I cleared the clutter of a week's work from my desk. We didn't see that the mailman had come and gone from our porch until Jack spotted a package through the glass-paned front door.

He brought me a box addressed in pencil, cursive letters slanting right. Lifting tape, I stripped away the brown-paper wrapping. Inside was an ancient, black, pressed-cardboard binder embossed with my grandfather's full name in gold letters. I ran my fingers over the cover. Flipping it open, I rested my eyes on a sheaf of onionskin pages. Crisp and professional looking, they must have been prepared by Grandma, who'd worked as a typist for thirty years—errors, if there were any, would have been lifted by the erasure tape in her trusted Selectric. She no longer used the manual 1942 Royal she still owned and that I'd tapped on as a kid, one clacking keystroke after another.

The first page, and the title, lay before me: "Accelerating Rotation Theory: An Exposition of the Development of the Earth."

Jack stuck his head into my office. His hair stood up in bunches, as it did when he'd been playing with Sammy. "How's Al's paper look?"

"Impressive."

"Why not bring it this weekend? Read it in the cabin."

"I don't dare take this anywhere. Jack, listen to this."

Night and day are generally thought of as passing around the Earth once during each period of rotation, which of course they do. Day remains always on the Earth's sunward side and night on its opposite dark hemisphere, which in fact they do. With this in mind, it is readily understood that the evolution of life, inseparable from the processes of erosion and sedimentation, occurred only on the Earth's sunlighted hemisphere until shortening of the day-night cycle established climatic conditions about as they are today.

"Wow," said Jack. "Make a copy. Got to run, we're trying to decide whether to pack Teddy or Piggy . . . "

I slipped the manuscript from the binder. Stacking it for my fax/copier, I didn't take my eyes off the machine as it worked. The copies came out dark but legible, black letters like lifebuoys against gray fog. I clicked the originals back into the binder and carried it with care to our fire safe. Our house deed, our family trusts, and my original book manuscripts were now joined by a discourse on a planet Grandpa supposed became itself through swifter and swifter rotation.

Over the weekend I felt drawn to those photocopies like a needle pulled north. The manuscript had the quality of creation myth, spun from unfamiliar language. My grandfather's words captivated me—it didn't matter that I couldn't grasp their meaning. After putting Sammy to bed, while an early snow brushed the windows of the cabin, I read passages to Jack.

In late pre-Cambrian time, through a process as yet unknown, forms of life materialized among the sediments on the floor of the primordial sea. Their fossilized remains are found in several unconformably deposited rock strata common to all of the continents. From this evidence, it is deduced that the Earth made several rotations during which time the primordial sea remained on its sunward side before the ocean basins were formed and into which the ancient sea gravitated.

Jack thought a minute. "Does it make sense to you?"

"It has such . . . authority. You want to believe him. But it sounds so unlikely."

"As in imaginary?" Jack reached up to draw a curtain over the whitening window. "Maybe call Joan next week? Al needs your help, and his time's short." He put his arms around me.

We curled together in bed, Jack's heartbeat steady against my back. As my mind slowed, I felt wrapped in the good fortune of a loving family and minimal drama, unlike the heroine in my novels. Brilliant about her work in forensics, biology, and anthropology, she'd have no problem dissecting the meaning of Grandpa's treatise with the sharpness of a Samurai sword. Her good thinking, however, wouldn't include keeping her personal life on track. That same heroine conducted a series of bad romances, was estranged from her parents, had a wayward daughter, and made no time for friends—in short, she lived a train-wreck of a life. It was more like the regular trauma I lived with in my river-guide years, before my friendship with Jack matured into love.

Monday descended, then evaporated in a slew of editorial calls. Evening settled before I could try Joan. When I did find a moment to telephone, she took time to review Grandpa's material with me. I read aloud:

Referring now specifically to animal life, certain invertebrates attained mobility and "marked time" among the sediments on the floor of that ancient sunward sea. The calcareous remains of their dead ancestors were carried, as on an endless belt, through the night environment of the Earth's opposite side. When that floor (the surface of any given continent) returned each time into the day environment, the nucleus of life which was marking time there had evolved and in some instances entirely new forms had appeared.

Joan coughed. "In a way, it's brilliant. He describes conveyer-belt transport as part of evolutionary design. But it's not the sea-floor spreading that's been well documented since the 1970s. There's no mention of plate tectonics."

"Does Grandpa even believe in plate tectonics?"

She hemmed. "He wouldn't be alone if he didn't. A few very accomplished researchers refute it. But I'm afraid he's barking up trees cut down a long time ago."

My heart took a dive.

Joan asked, "Are you there?"

"Yeah." My voice came out small, an echo from the summers of my youth. Over all a quiet but vital grandfather had presided in sun hat, fishing vest, and rubber boots.

My mother and I said goodbye. I carried Grandpa's treatise to the living room, where Jack and Sammy were finishing a game of Rummy. Sammy applauded when he saw the binder. "Great-Grandpa's story! Can we read it for bedtime?"

I shook my head. "It's still being worked on."

"Please!" Sammy jumped up.

"It's not a good kid's book."

"I'm not a kid!" All four feet of my son were bouncing with excitement.

Jack held his cards near his chin, his eyes on me.

"Well. Only if you're in bed in a flash, Sammy-O." I fanned my fingers in our signal meaning *five minutes*. He ran to brush his teeth.

Jack set down his Rummy hand. "What'd Joan say?"

"That Al has missed the boat. No pun intended."

"It's not good science?"

"I imagine it's the absolute best a woodworker-slash-fisherman living in a town of one thousand can do with references from the public library."

Jack frowned. "What's next?"

"I have to tell Al something. But I don't know what." I kissed Jack's standing-up hair and took the binder into Sammy's room. Settling on the bed, I reclined with my son on his pillows. He clutched his stuffed pig, his little chest rising and falling from his having rushed through his nighttime routine. I opened Grandpa's binder to the introduction. "You ready?"

"Of course!"

"Here's something from near the beginning. 'There came a time when some amphibians'—that means frogs and newts—"

"Duh."

"'. . . evolved to an existence entirely terrestrial.' That means they moved from living in the ocean to being on land."

"Wow!"

"'Some of the reptiles—you know, snakes and lizards—"

"Double duh."

"Sorry. '. . . attained improved means and methods of mobilization.' He's saying they could walk around pretty well once they became land creatures."

Sammy raised one hand in the air.

"Yes, Sammy?"

"Great-Grandpa Al is smart, isn't he, Mom?"

"Very."

My all-knowing son sat up, nowhere near sleepy. "Mom, what's 'evolved'?"

Two days later I arrived home from grocery shopping to a ringing phone. I hurried to my office in time to hear the message machine recording, ". . . his number at the hospital is . . ."

I picked up. "Grandma?"

"There you are, Mare. It's that pain again. He was out with Chuck gathering hickory nuts until his chest hurt. Got 'tighter than a table vise,' he said. He came home wheezing like our fireplace bellows. *Eeh-haw. Eeh-haw.* I took him to Dansville. Your mother knows."

I'd visited the massive brick Noyes Hospital in Dansville only once, when I was twelve or so. Joan and I had gone to see ninety-eight-year-old Auntie Gev, who'd lost the desire to eat or drink. Her chin-length hair was paper white, and her clear, blue gaze reminded me of creek water. The biggest clue she was failing was her voice, which possessed far more air than sound. My mother had to lean in to hear as I watched the green of the trees outside the window and wondered how soon we could leave.

Now, when I telephoned Grandpa's room, he spoke with that same hush Gev had all those years ago. "They're running a few more tests on me. Then I'm going home."

"You take it easy. Don't do the Grandpa thing and act all . . . stubborn."

He chuckled, then gasped as if struck. I waited as he labored to breathe.

When his discomfort passed, I said, "Grandpa, I read your treatise. It's very well written. Jack and Sammy like it, too."

"Can you . . . do anything with it?" His breath ebbed and flowed.

"Well, it's so good, but so technical."

"Right, girl. That's where you come in."

"You mean interpret it?" I sighed. "I doubt I can. It's . . . beyond my abilities."

Silence. Then, "Well, you can have the boat anyway." His handset rocked and scrabbled on the cradle before settling in.

A recording came on, telling me to hang up if I'd like to make a call. My thoughts first ran cool with indignation then warm with a desire to perform some brilliant feat of rescue. I dialed my grandmother. She listened to my bruised account of Grandpa's dismissal, then asked, "Is it publishable, Mare?"

"Well . . . "

"Ah," she said. "You know, he sent it to S_____ *Magazine* a few years ago. It took them months to respond."

"And?"

"They sent a letter back saying his idea had no merit whatsoever." Her thin voice shook. "They didn't have to say that. It was just—mean. He was so mad he didn't speak for days. Oh, he'd shut me out before, but not for years."

"Now I'm in for the silent treatment."

"Yes." She paused. "Mare, I wish people knew how hard he's worked. Twenty years, off and on. Reading late at night, passing weekends at the library . . . he's been at it far longer than the average person spends in college."

"Or even getting a doctorate."

"Oh?" She chuckled as she did when she hadn't quite heard. "You know, he's very intelligent. He would've been an important man out West if he hadn't been called home."

"Out West? When?"

"During the Depression. You didn't know?" Her words came bit by bit, pulled out of deep memory. My grandfather had helped survey the last unmapped sections of the Grand Canyon, Arizona, and Mount Lassen, California. He had a letter of commendation from the U.S. Geological Survey. "Major Dutton signed it himself," said Grandma. "I still have the letter upstairs. I wish S_____ Magazine knew that."

Then my great-grandfather—to me just a face in a sepia-toned photograph—demanded his third son come home. If the whole family didn't help on the farm, they'd lose the land. My great-grandfather claimed the loss would be on Al's head.

"That hit him hard," said Grandma, who'd grown up on the farm next door. "It wasn't fair. We should never ask such things of our children."

The next day I spoke with my agent. "Victoria, who do we know at S_____ Magazine?"

"Nobody, but I can find someone who does. What's up?"

"I want to place a story on their back page."

"Mare, the back page? I'm pretty sure they don't do fiction."

"This is different. I have a . . . piece on family. Can you call me if it's a go?"

"Absolutely."

Next I dialed the hospital. When I reached Grandpa's room,

Joan answered. She'd flown to Rochester, driven to Dansville, and was at his bedside. "He's sleeping now," she whispered.

"I have to talk to him. It's his exposition. I have an idea for it—to get it in print. But it would be different, a little. What I need to know is, would it be okay to give it a new twist?"

"Yes. Yes, I'm sure it would. But Mare, he's very sick."

"How sick?"

"He's got cancer—lung cancer. And he's refusing treatment."

The words fell hard, a tower toppling.

Joan continued, "He's probably not going home."

My mind went to memories of muggy summer days, with barbecues near warm ponds. My cousins and I swam with our feet held high to avoid the muddy bottom and the leeches we were certain were there. We played dress-up with Grandma's steamer trunks of dress-up clothes, racked up countless games of dominoes, and rushed around the lawns that surrounded my grandparents' big, wood-frame house until fireflies traced ephemeral loops in the dark.

"Mare? Your grandfather says you're to receive his guideboat. 'No arguments,' he told me."

"But—"

"The doctor just arrived. Sorry, hon, got to run. Talk later?"

Leaving my office, I crossed through the house to our bedroom, fell on the bed, and wept into an afghan Grandma had crocheted for a wedding present. By the time Jack brought Sammy home, I hadn't moved. My husband and son stood in the doorway, puzzled looks on their faces. Then Sammy ran to watch a cartoon while Jack started a pizza baking.

Jack returned to sit with me, his hazel eyes as dark as they get. With his mouth set in a line, he listened to my news. He asked, "Can you fly there this week?"

"Yeah. I'll check for tickets . . . first thing tomorrow."

He rubbed my back. "What's happening with S_____?"

"Victoria thinks she can get me in. I want to adapt a piece from his ... " I resumed weeping.

Jack reached an arm around me. "Mare, babe, you need dinner. Come on. Pizza's ready."

After picking at my meal, I roamed the house, looking out windows into our circle of woods. It had been a dry winter. Our garden lay bare and hummocky from light snows that had melted without sticking. I closed my eyes. When I reopened them, I considered the indoor furniture: a drop-leaf table and chairs made by Grandpa; a recipe box built of his signature cherry wood; a walking cane carved from a pine branch he'd collected. In my office, two pictures of him stood on my bookshelf. One showed him linking arms with Grandma on their fiftieth wedding anniversary, she tiny and wearing a sky-blue cardigan over her shoulders, he heads higher in a short-sleeved cotton shirt. In the second photo, Grandpa strolled through red-and-yellow woods by the Genesee River. He wore his fall coat and flannel-lined khaki pants. Anyone who didn't know him would think he was just a random old man closing the distance.

Letting my hand roam the spines of books, I pulled *Extinction* from my shelf. I opened it, by chance coming to this passage near the middle:

It wasn't that the birds were gone that turned her off to the human race; it was that we had killed them. Ivory-Billed Woodpeckers had only wanted a chance to further their DNA and raise their young in a couple of swamps in Louisiana. In the game of survival of the fittest, they held a losing hand. Now some murderer was out there, targeting ornithologists who protected the Ivory Bill legacy, and she intended to find him or die trying.

I slapped the book shut.

Sitting at my desk, I took up my notebook and favorite roller-ball pen. I flipped through Grandpa's binder, searching for key words: *changes, processes, transformation. Exposition.* Sketching circles and curves in my notebook, I let my scribbling develop into phrases, then sentences. On the page in front of me, a story was taking shape.

In the morning, Grandpa's voice on the phone came from a faraway place. Even as he murmured, I heard stubbornness in the rising inflection of his sentences. "No chemo for me," he said.

My blood raced. "But . . . you said we have to stick with it. Year after year."

He let out the world's weariest sigh.

"Remember that loon?" I asked. "What happened to 'we have to persevere constantly'?"

"I have been." His voice was as faint as a light breeze. "All my life."

"Grandpa. My agent is getting your—our work—into S_____ *Magazine.*" I wanted to add, "those bastards," but did not.

"Good girl. We'll be coauthors."

"I'm flying out to see you tomorrow."

"Do," he said. "Bring your family, Mare. You can take them out in the boat."

We finished our call, and I stared out the window at the blue Utah sky. A wisp of cloud gathered over mountains to the east. After several minutes, I wiped my damp eyes with both shirtsleeves before turning on my computer. Calling up a new document, I drummed my fingers on the edge of the keyboard, thinking. With time, a technical paper might evolve from my grandfather's manuscript. Meanwhile I would write the kind of prose I knew best.

Sammy wandered in, wearing Grandma's crocheted afghan as a cape. "Mom, can I—what are you doing?

"Typing a story. Great-Grandpa Al's story."

"From his book? That beginning part?"

"Not really. This starts more in the middle. It takes place in the wild West when there were no maps yet, just giant birds and bears and big villages of really wise native people."

"What about Great-Grandpa?"

"He climbed unclimbed mountains and crossed untamed rivers with other daring explorers."

"Cool!"

Sammy ran off, appearing to be satisfied with my answer and forgetting whatever he'd come in to ask. I typed through the day, taking no breaks except for dinner, returning to my desk after dark. While I drafted sentences and shaped paragraphs, I heard Jack's voice carrying through the house—no doubt spinning bedtime tales for Sammy about our son's new favorite subject, Great-Grandpa the hero. Even after the murmur of storytelling had ended and Jack had gone to bed himself, the words poured out of me onto the page. As I wrote late, my lamp no doubt illuminated the only work in progress in Utah that included a guideboat, an important man from Geneseo, and an exposition of the development of the Earth.

Endangered Species

If I were to make a study of the tracks of animals and represent them by plates, I should conclude with the tracks of man.

—Henry David Thoreau

The Pomeranian next door turned prey in an instant. One minute its yapping hovered near Tom's consciousness, the next the dog squealed as if skewered and went silent. Terror filled the momentary high-pitched scream, cut off mid breath. Anybody out doing yard work, as Tom was, would've heard it. Certainly the birds did—crows cawed up from the big Doug-fir. They flushed and settled again, and the sunset-pink air grew quiet. Tom froze in place, a wave of his brown hair covering his eyes. When he heard nothing more, he checked over the fence but saw only his neighbor Martin's perfect green lawn, potted pink geraniums, and hot tub protected with padded red top.

Hours after the dog's disappearance, Martin returned from dinner out at La Vie. Tom heard him call for his pet at the back steps, but there was no answer, not even the pig-like snuffles the dog made when excited. The Pomeranian had been in the habit of wandering to the creek edging both properties, and Martin called again at the creekbank. Still no reply.

"Tom, my man." Martin peered at him through the small gap between their fences. "Is Pommie with you by any chance?"

"Haven't seen him."

From a distance, Martin looked younger than his sixty-two years, but up close, his true age was more obvious due to facial skin stretching beyond its normal elasticity and the sharp boundary between his auburn hair dye and white sideburns. When they'd met, Martin had confided to Tom that he'd "just had his eyes done" and played golf to keep fit so he could date women thirty years his junior. "In other words, around your age, my man, though I'm no longer as handsome as you."

Martin retreated inside, and Tom resumed hacking the bay laurel grown out of control. He was getting the northern California home his parents had left him ready to sell. When his mother had fallen ill, he'd driven up from Vegas for what he thought would be a long visit. Instead she passed on within days, followed a month later by his father who hadn't been healthy for years. Tom proceeded to take care of details, all the while missing his folks as well as his wife, Sue, who'd just filed for divorce after a long separation.

In the morning Martin reported his dog missing to the Pets Ahoy Animal Shelter, as well as the sheriff's office. Both warned that there'd been recent mountain lion sightings and he should call Fish and Game to note the incident. Martin did, then let Tom know a warden would come out in the afternoon. Tom didn't hesitate. He took his little digital point-and-shoot to the creek to look for tracks. He'd hunted when he was younger but lately made the move from Remington to Canon. Although he'd lost the urge to kill, he still liked the stealth needed to close in on wildlife and capture their beauty.

Tom skirted the fence line to the channel. The ground felt

dry and firm until he reached the water. There the bed gave way underfoot, muddy and soft, and the air smelled of wet earth. The creek trickled at its October low—not much flow before the rains started for the season.

Years earlier, he'd walked the creek up into the hills. Less than a mile from his parents' back gate, he found dark redwood groves and deep stands of oak draped with lichen. The woods were untamed, unplanned—perfect to Tom's eyes. Tumbling over falls, the creek descended ledges of black rock. Up there he found sharp-edged deer prints, heron tracks scrabbled in the mud, and raccoon scat full of crawdad shells. Along the creek he felt a rare peace. It reminded him of the hushed sanctuary of the church he and Sue had attended on the north coast.

Down in town, though—behind Martin's house—the stream channel was cased in concrete. A row of Italian cypress lined Martin's long, paved driveway, which crossed a walk-through steel culvert. Nearby, fractured bedrock allowed a spring to pour out among fern and monkey flower. Martin had built a holding pool, square and stylish, to accent the clarity of the fresh water. No doubt the pool attracted wildlife despite its intended purpose, which was, as Martin said, "to astonish his out-of-town guests."

Now, carrying his camera, Tom spotted what he was looking for among the patches of stream gravel: a single animal print, no less than six inches across, four splayed toe pads in an impression as detailed as a plaster cast. The fifth and central pad resembled a flattened human nose—rounded with two wings flaring like nostrils. The whole thing was deep, pressed into the mud with authority. There were no claws showing.

Lion print. Still filling with water. If it was the predator who'd attacked Pommie, it had come back.

Tom acted fast, snapping photos, making sure to capture the print near his own foot for scale. When he'd documented it to his satisfaction, he looked for others. Nothing. It appeared the animal had moved on hard bedrock when it could. Tom used his toe to scrape some pebbles over the single track as well as his own footprints—with care, to leave no trace.

A breeze brought the pungent smell of soaked fur. More scent came, strong and rank: big cat odor? Tom's heart pumped with excitement, but he also felt the fear of being prey. He made himself as big as possible by raising his jacket above his head and singing Green Day songs so loud his chest rattled. It took him about half a minute to back downstream and scramble up the bank to his garden.

Later that day, the Fish and Game warden arrived and stood with Tom and Martin at the streambank. A tall man with a tan uniform, orange safety vest, and shaved head, he hunkered near the Italian cypress and gave advice. "Don't go down there alone. And never at dawn or dusk, when predators hunt. You don't want to run into one—no way, no how."

Martin asked, "What about my Pommie?"

The warden shook his head. "Sorry, sir. If it was a lion, it's protected—an endangered species." He handed Martin a brochure entitled *Living in Cougar Country*.

Martin snorted.

The warden eyed him. "I'll check back in a week or so. Or you can call me anytime. Name's Brad." He handed them each his business card. "And don't worry. More people are hit by lightning than killed by lions. You follow the advice in that pamphlet, you'll be fine."

Tom returned to the kitchen at his folks' place, where he'd set up his laptop. For a minute he thought about not printing the photos he'd taken of the animal track. As he deliberated, the phone rang, and it was Martin. He'd just invited his "woman friend" to visit from Los Angeles. He couldn't stand to be alone,

"especially with Pommie gone. It's been terrible, just terrible."
Trudy, a freelance portrait photographer, would arrive in a few
days. "You two will have a lot to talk about, both being artists
of the lens."

"But I'm just an amateur."

"Never mind that. You're good at everything—your dear
old folks, rest their souls, told me so." Martin lowered his voice,
as if anyone would be listening. "Confidentially, Tom, I hope
to marry Trudy. But I haven't asked yet. She's younger and still
busy with her career."

Tom congratulated Martin and said goodbye. He sat down
to print out just one photo of the animal track. Then he spent
the afternoon clearing more of the unpruned growth out back.

Over the next two days, Tom observed Martin sparing no
effort tidying up his yard for Trudy's arrival. His mow-and-
blow guy came to do the lawn, but instead of ignoring him as
he usually did, Martin directed the rewrapping of his Italian
cypress in mist nets from the lowest branches to the conical
tops. When finished, the trees in silhouette looked like dark-
green, narrow-headed people.

In the evenings Tom read the local websites online. The
Journal-Tribune had run a series on local wildlife, and readers
had posted more than thirty comments. Landowners on several
hillside properties had seen "a large creature, moving fast"
and a "tawny animal that jumped the fence." The comments
culminated at the bottom of the webpage with this one:

Dear Editor,

We live on the creek and personally observe wild animals
from the surrounding hills using the waterway as a sort of
"sidewalk" into town. This would be fine except some are
fierce predators that will stop at nothing to get their needs
met. I've already lost my beloved pet to some stalking
beast. It could just as well have been a small child carried

off! Then wouldn't the community be in an uproar! Now there are reports of mountain lions roaming the hills. A coincidence? I think not! My question to city officials is, how far will you let this problem go before you act?

Sincerely, Martin Banks

Tom's heart beat hard as he considered responding with what he knew.

Later that day Martin brought Trudy over with her camera. Her blonde hair shone in the sunshine, and her light brown eyes showed mixed excitement and embarrassment. The color in her cheeks deepened as Martin made introductions. A moment later he excused himself to return a phone call to an "Indiana Jones type" who was going to help with something.

Trudy hoisted her camera. "Mind if I . . . ?"

Tom shrugged.

She snapped pictures of the ash grove, of the maple losing its leaves, and of Tom ripping English ivy off an oak tree, where the vine had taken hold. "This place feels so natural," she said.

Tom nodded. "My parents put in only native plants. And they never used any chemicals. They were . . . " His voice caught. ". . . ahead of their time."

She gave him a sympathetic look, then checked her camera. "Here," she said, showing him the digital viewer. He looked first out of politeness and then from real interest. Each of her shots was insightful. There were close-ups of leaf patterns, wide-angle views of plant assemblages with the artistry of mosaics, and details of Doug-fir cones scattered on homebuilt rock walls.

"You've got a good eye," Tom said, as Martin returned.

Martin beamed and tapped his forehead. "Vision. It's what

Trudy brings to the *table*."

"Oh, Martin." Trudy sighed.

"I'm serious," he said. "Only you could find beauty in this overgrown jungle."

She blushed again. "It is beautiful. And it's not a jungle."

Martin put an arm around her shoulders and aimed her home. Tom didn't look up from his ivy pulling until they'd reached their back steps. Martin entered the house before Trudy, pulling her in after him when she paused to snap his container plantings of French lavender and Russian sage. Tom hoped she'd glance back at him before going inside. She didn't.

Trudy returned alone the next afternoon, slipping unannounced through the gap between the fences. "Martin was called away on last-minute business." She adjusted her camera to hang down her back before kneeling to help pull weeds. "The money was too good to pass up." When she continued working without gloves, Tom offered his.

She took them and peered at him. "Martin doesn't garden. He hires somebody to help. But you probably knew that."

They worked side by side, Tom silent, Trudy humming. Her nearness made him feel light headed. He counted the months since Sue had left him over that mess with the stripper from the Sapphire in Vegas. Eleven months—almost a year. Christ.

When the sun dropped near the hills, Trudy straightened up and removed the gloves. "Have you seen the creature Martin thinks got Pommie?"

"No." Tom didn't look up from his work.

"Was it a mountain lion, do you think?"

He shrugged.

She persisted. "I'd like to see it."

He stopped weeding. Her shining eyes excited him, but he tried not to let it show. No way he'd reveal much to any woman again, ever, not since he'd begged his wife to come back, with no success. He'd driven to that desert town where Sue worked and said he'd take all the blame. Who knew he'd leave their home on the coast, hit the blue skies of Nevada, and lose all sense? But Sue had said he'd made his bed and could damn well lie in it.

Tom eyed Trudy. "You wouldn't want to be closer to any predator than . . . well, than your rooftop."

"Great idea! I'll get the ladder."

He followed her as if sleepwalking to Martin's double-car garage, where her Volkswagen beetle was parked by itself. He retrieved the extension ladder as she directed and leaned it against the back gutter of Martin's house. She giggled. "Martin wouldn't do this." She preceded Tom up the ladder and over the gutter, and he held the rungs, watching her camera swing above her jeans as she climbed. Once she reached the roof, she held the top of the ladder for him. Her grip was firm, solid.

From the sloping asphalt shingles, they had a clear view of an unclouded western horizon. A strip of gold lingered over the hills. Upstream of Martin's cypress and spring, the creek wound out of sight. Trudy snapped photo after photo; Tom pulled out his camera for a few shots, too. He got some good ones of her bright-toothed, almost maniacal joy.

Dark settled. Stars followed in a moonless sky. "I'm not afraid of the predator," said Trudy. "Whatever it is. But Martin really fears it."

"He should."

She laughed. "Serious?"

Tom shrugged.

"You're so funny," she said. "Not like anyone else I know."

The air grew colder, with a hint of marine layer drifting

in from the coast. Tom and Trudy sat close but not touching until they agreed it was time to go back down. She retreated to Martin's big house on a path well illuminated with sensor lights. Tom guessed he could go with her, but he didn't. He followed his parents' narrow walkway through the unlit native garden and inside to the old hide-a-bed.

Over the next two evenings, with Martin detained by business, Tom and Trudy climbed to the roof again. The second night's sky resembled the first, clear and mild followed by a slow chill. Trudy brought a fleece throw and Tom was glad she did, because the damp, cool air entered his bones. He recalled that same feeling from the years he and Sue had spent on the coast. White tufts of fog hung on the western hills, sunlight cutting the mist tops as if slicing smoke. Oaks rattled in the wind down by the creek and, as darkness came on, the black tree limbs framed by gray evening faded into night.

"It's beautiful," she said. "Those sun rays looked like heaven."

"Uh-huh. Bet you and your camera captured it."

She kissed his right ear. "What I want to capture is the predator."

He turned to her. They lay back in each other's arms.

"We should go in," she said. "Together."

"Your fiancé wouldn't like that."

"Fiancé? More like sugar daddy." She giggled.

Again they slept apart, and again they rendezvoused the next evening. This time they spent sunset on the roof wrapped in Tom's Hudson Bay blanket. They traded just a few more words about Martin. "He hates the predator," she said, hand on Tom's belly.

"He shouldn't. It's just a lone animal coming to the spring."

She stiffened. "Martin's spring?"

Tom pulled away. "I'm only guessing." He waited a few

minutes before suggesting they call it a night.

The next morning, she joined him in the back garden, where he was picking native blackberries. Her hair stood out in bunches, and her eyes had small, dark rings. "You're killing me, Tom."

He stopped his work. "How?"

"Why won't you come inside?"

"I'm still married. And you almost are."

She focused on a berry as if it held an answer. "They're so filled with dark juice." She looked up and ran her tongue over her lips.

Tom went back to foraging. "Tell Martin."

"Damn you." Her voice was low and soft as the creek flow.

"Seriously. He listens to you. Maybe you could get him to plant native berries in place of those silly cypress. And your lawn over there—"

"Martin's."

"Whoever's. It's got no value. It's just useless and thirsty."

She picked at the berries. "You know, Martin mentioned your time in Las Vegas."

"What about it?"

"Just that you weren't with your wife there. That you might as well be divorced."

"Uh-huh. Well, tell him to leave the spring alone. The raccoons and deer and lion need it."

"Lion?" She reached a cool hand behind his neck and pulled him in for a kiss. It started out soft and turned urgent and hard. After a minute he stood back and led her without touching into his parents' house. Caution slowed his steps, but he kept going. He wanted her. They spent the day indoors, under the Hudson Bay blanket on the hide-a-bed. Out of her jeans, she was plumper than he'd imagined, but her flesh was ripe and delicious. In his arms, under him, she came again and again, a wild, abandoned look in her eyes. Throughout it all—penetration, climax, release—he stayed watchful, a lens aimed at his own lovemaking and her liberation.

Martin's return coincided with a bout of early winter rains. Tom woke the morning after his time with Trudy to see Martin's big Lexus parked next to her Volkswagen. Tom stood at his kitchen window, waiting. Either Martin or Trudy or both should arrive at the front door soon, demanding or giving some kind of confession.

Neither showed. Rain soaked everything in Tom's backyard, from the thick-branched bigleaf maple to the delicate snowberry. Puddles grew into ponds on the dirt footpaths as the rain sluiced to earth. In a daze, Tom startled when the phone rang at noon. He jumped for the call.

It was a man, his parents' realtor. "The neighbor next door wants the house. Do you know Martin Banks? He said he knows you. He's buying it for his girlfriend." The papers were all in order, already signed and awaiting countersignature. Tom's throat tightened.

"By the way," said the realtor, "the only thing Mr. Banks didn't approve was the Native Flora and Fauna clause. He wants to replace the garden."

Tom managed to say he'd think about it, but after he hung up his anger grew. Pulling out his father's big black umbrella, throwing on a parka, he hurried down the front path. The rain fell in torrents. He rushed toward Martin's yard, reached the front walkway, and—kept going.

Tom followed the creek to the hills, first taking the sidewalks, then climbing up the channels. In the deep of the woods, the rain couldn't penetrate the canopy of redwood, oak, and fir. He closed the umbrella and tucked it under his arm, the green overstory a shield over him. Among wet fern, tree bark, and earth, he spent the afternoon following a lone pileated woodpecker along the creek, hopping boulders to cross where it crossed, stopping to rest when it paused, listening as it pummeled the bark of a Doug-fir or bay.

After the woodpecker lost him in a line of redwood trees, and the day's light dulled, Tom headed home. He felt a satisfied exhaustion from wandering. Who needed a native plant clause? There were woods right up the street. He'd call the realtor to set up a time to sign.

Moments after arriving home and getting out of his wet clothes, wearing only a towel around his waist, he heard tapping at the front door. He swung it open. "Trudy?" He was met by a burst of high-pitched yapping: a small, white dog strained at a red leash held by a grim-faced Martin in a trench coat and tweed rainhat.

Tom forced a grin. "Hey! Is that . . . ?"

"Pommie. Turned up at Pets Ahoy." Scowling at Tom's bare chest and legs, Martin tossed a manila envelope on the floor. He hustled away without a word, his trench coat collar pulled up, his shoulders hunched, his little dog growling before it trotted alongside.

Tom retrieved the envelope, slid it onto the kitchen counter, and stood back from it. He paced, keeping his distance, until, at last, he reached for the envelope and broke the seal. Inside were two glossy, eight-by-ten photographs. At first he couldn't make them out: even with an obviously expert use of light, the shots had come out dark. Taken today during the rainstorm, he supposed. As he stared, he recognized human shapes framed by the culvert under Martin's driveway.

In the first picture, a tall, rough-looking man held a rifle. It was a 30-06, a caliber Tom knew from his hunting days. He'd never used a weapon with a silencer, though, as this one had—a canister longer and more narrow than a beer can. The hunter wore an Indiana Jones style fedora and camouflage jacket. At his feet lay an animal as big as a man, soft edged, and limp. The creek, beginning to swell with the rains, braided around the fallen beast and the hunter's rubber boots.

In a second photograph, Martin stood beside the hunter, now squatting and holding the animal by its neck. Stretched to afford a full view, the prey had pointed cat ears, long tail, and shaggy underbelly. Its wide paws more than six inches across rested in curls, the authority gone out of them. Martin's tan cheeks offset a white-toothed, thin-lipped smile.

Tom sunk to his knees on the shaggy carpet in the living room. He'd never broken down after Sue left, or when they lost their home on the north coast, or even when his parents passed. But now he sobbed on the floor, photo beside him, his belly hurting as if he'd been punched.

In the backyard the next morning, Tom walked the paths in his folks' garden. He felt empty, poured out. Still, he'd pulled a few things together, now contained in two nine-by-twelve manila envelopes he held under one arm. He'd also packed his bags to leave. In the new light, he surveyed the manzanita borders—all pruned during his work over the past weeks. The toyons and madrones had been cleaned of dead branches. They looked natural but cared for, which was what he'd come to do. The house and garden would show well now.

He didn't dare even glance at Martin's house, but with his peripheral vision he saw a light on upstairs. Perhaps a bathroom, off a master suite Martin shared with Trudy? Tom didn't know. He had never been inside; nor did he figure ever to go there. In a moment he couldn't stop himself looking, and he made out a silhouette framed by bright, fluorescent light.

Too small a shape to be Martin's. He thought about calling up to Trudy, but the window was closed. Was she humming to herself? Or looking in the mirror into animal eyes? The light shut off. Just as well—he couldn't be certain of what he'd say if they were to speak.

He could mention the house, he supposed. He planned to stop by the realtor's office on his way out of town. Might as well keep the place listed—another buyer would approve the Native Flora and Fauna clause. No reason to jump at the first offer. There was no hurry now, after all.

Tom strolled to the creekbank. The flow had swollen with rains, running high and muddy enough to cover the hunter's tracks. The streambed would show no trace of what had happened in Martin's culvert. As Tom stood listening to the rush of current, he fingered the envelopes. The first held a few of his point-and-shoot pictures: one of the lion track with time and date stamp, one of a glorious, happy Trudy up on Martin's roof, the sun in her hair.

The light came on again upstairs at Martin's. Tom held his breath as the window opened. It was Trudy. She met his gaze. His vision adjusted, and he made out a gleam of anger in her eyes. Anger? No, something else. A wild longing? She slammed the window shut but not before Tom caught the high-pitched bark of the Pomeranian from somewhere in the house.

What a waste. He was glad he'd be posting the first envelope with his photos within the hour. Martin and Trudy would receive it the next day.

The second envelope held the hunting photos, which Tom had marked with Martin's name and phone number. This mailing was addressed to Brad, the Fish and Game warden. The agency would want to know the fate of one of its protected species. Martin and Trudy had done a beautiful job of documenting the demise of the lion—Tom needed only to pass the information along. And he'd kept copies of everything, because he'd be sure to follow up sometime after he'd wandered back up the coast. His universe of big trees and flowing streams might be shrinking, but he'd still go there. It was still home.

Steelies

No one listened when I warned about the water. The valley people, I mean. They always gave me the same empty looks, like nothing I said was new or true, and these mindless nods, no better than bobble-headed dolls. Like, "We're not about to stop pumping out of the creeks, so give it a rest, fish lady." That's what they called me—fish lady—and worse, probably, because I told them that sucking up water doesn't drain just the streambeds. You stand to lose everything: first the summer pools, then the wet river cobbles and wells, then the last, mighty fish named for the silver-blue dress they put on to spawn.

But why take my word for it? Anyone could follow me and see for himself. Brad was the only one who did, the only one who said he'd be there and then made sure he showed up. He asked to tour the creeks with me as part of his job for Fish and Game. I agreed, thinking he might be able to do something about all the hoses sucking water from the summer pools like straws.

When I first met Brad at the Fuller Creek confluence, an alarm went off in me. He was standing on the bank upstream of the cement plant, questioning the homeless men under the MLK Jr. Avenue Bridge. He wore a tan uniform and a cap that I later learned covered a shaved head. His warden's badge caught the sun. He looked official, making notes. As I drove up, all I could think was he'd better not run those guys off—they make some of the best fish sightings in the valley from their streamside camp.

When I walked within earshot, I heard Jerry, the tall, gray-haired leader, filling Brad in about the flooding earlier in the season. Three days of solid rains back in April had swollen the creeks into muddy messes. Jerry and crew had been forced to move their furniture up the bank to keep it dry. While doing so Jerry noticed the backs of steelhead swimming upstream through the high water. Now the creek had fallen again and their couch was back at streamside, missing two of its three cushions. Curtis and Stoner, Jerry's two regular sidekicks, lay propped on elbows in the dirt just above the high-water mark, half-covered in sleeping bags. They all called me "fish lady," too, but in a nice way I didn't mind.

Brad asked Jerry if he'd ever seen any landowners siphoning the creek. Jerry pointed his thumb at me. "Ask R.J. She knows." Brad closed the cover on his metal clipboard and, for the first time, gave me his full attention. He looked me over head to toe—thinking who knows what—while I squirmed as I did in the presence of an official. And a handsome one, too, around my age. He took in my rubber boots, my notebook and pen, and my long, silver hair—it had been getting that way since I was twenty-two. He didn't hesitate. He invited me to his state truck for a bottle of spring water.

Back in the Fish and Game six-pack, the first breeze of the afternoon crept through Brad's lowered windows. He poured cool water into my canteen. "You've seen spawners in the watershed, the males and females?"

I nodded.

"Even digging their redds? Actually nesting?"

"Of course." Surely he knew the fish were still here. The doe prepares the gravels, and the buck guards her, ready to release milt over her eggs. Just like in the textbooks. Usually the buck is battling the stray rainbows—young punks, you could say—who try to be first to the female. While the males fight to claim the streambed, the doe twirls, really graceful, as if she were born to dance. An acrobat.

Brad's eyes shone. "How about taking me to their spawning sites sometime?"

An electric current ran through me, but I don't think it showed. He didn't ask me about the hoses and water withdrawals, which I admit gave me pause. Didn't anyone but me care if the fish had the flow they needed?

Early evening I returned home to a message on my phone machine from a local poet. He read a few lines from Rilke that ended with, "Within yourself, you one-time-child, within yourself." That's all I caught of it. "R.J., I hope you'll consider saying yes this time. Do call back." I erased the message.

The classical hour played on the radio as I typed up the day's notes. I hadn't seen any steelhead, but they're good at hiding. I'd started my tracking up at Fox Creek, where the pools swirl in bedrock under the redwoods. The streams at the top of the watershed run cool and clear, dark in the shadows, light in the sun. Swallows wheel down from over the treetops, chasing some hatch or other, caddis flies mostly. And the creeks sometimes hold a lot of baby steelhead, or fry as they're called, with oval parr marks on their sides that look like flattened water beetles. Those tiny fish, just starting life, are the ones I call steelies. They're the creatures the valley philistines say are "small enough to live in a puddle, so what's the big deal, fish lady?"

Every time I make notes about the headwaters, I follow the main stream down the valley, past vineyards, past the dairies. Everywhere a tributary enters, like Miwok or Orchard or Lincoln, I stop to look for fish, to find which creeks they run in. And I record what I see, like: "Two spawners holding in riffle on Embrazos Creek. Good shelter, gravel clean. Half-hour mating dance. No eggs yet."

In the south, where I end my route every afternoon, the creeks are warm and murky. The trash fish—pikeminnows and such—sit around waiting to lunch on the second-year steelhead on their way out to sea. The pikeminnows are native, too, but I find them heinous. They're nothing like the high-minded steelies, who want their water clear and cold on a summer day. Their epic journey to sea followed by their return to find clean mating gravels strikes me as the height of love.

As I worked at my desk, Mahler's Fourth Symphony came on. I stopped to focus on the music as it took forever to climax. The strings drew out the melody while the woodwinds pranced to the rhythm of sleigh bells in the percussion section. Sleigh bells! I wandered to my open window. In the forest behind my backyard, the oaks had leafed out. The buckeyes, too, were green and tender, with flowered spikes in bloom: creamy blossoms, waving in the breeze, limber and reaching up. The music built, with the horns coming in like streams feeding a river, until everything flowed together and I couldn't tell one instrument from the next.

I returned to my notes, my attention still on the orchestra. It poured out a crescendo, a flood of music with all the instruments playing in unison. They ended in three abrupt, ear-pounding chords. Then it was over. The words on the page blurred through the tears in my eyes. Again the window drew me—in the evening light, the buckeye blooms glowed and swayed. I thought of Brad in his tan pants and how they might look if his own spike were stiff in them. My God. Here I'd just met him, and I was already having thoughts of pollination. Perhaps I'd been alone too long and dwelling too much on the mating of fish.

That was just it. What I needed was a man who could fill the creek to overflowing. I hadn't tried partnering since my husband, Bob, had followed his dream to Maui to manage a dive shop. He'd wanted me to go with him, but I didn't think I could abandon the steelies.

But why not, really? What good was I doing touring around the watershed spying on steelies like some kind of fish pervert?

That night I lay in bed with the sweats, my body hot as a frying potato, my skin wet and slick. My doctor had said that the night heat comes from the change of life, which wasn't far off for me. Whatever, but those flashes reminded me of the juvenile steelhead baking on the summer cobbles. They'd be there soon, out in the drawn-down creeks, stranded with not-enough water. And I'd be here, lying above the sheets, covered in way too much.

Brad didn't get back in touch for nine months. I'd been desperate for his help with the fish right away, but June turned to July without a word, then summer to autumn. Some steelies had taken shelter in the cool pools up in the headwaters, but many more were not so fortunate. There was nothing to do but record the numbers dying in the hot streambeds and pray Brad would help bring the power of the government to bear on their life-and-death struggles. When he didn't show, I despaired over the losses. I even phoned Bob in Lahaina and sobbed, and he begged me to come join him at the dive shop. He'd been lonely over there, he said, and even the fish had mates, didn't they?

Before I could find the right plane ticket on Maui Air, though, winter came on, wet and exciting. Mature fish were turning up like lost coins throughout the watershed. I stopped searching for air passage. Driving my route took a turn for the best as I counted adults who'd arrived to start a new batch of steelies. Valiant fish—like bees reclaiming a cleaned-out hive. My heart raced in their presence.

The big storms passed. The new year came. One clear February morning, I sat on a boulder near Esperanza Creek, making notes. A pair of mallards dabbled in an eddy beyond the willows, and the stream sang over its bed. Blackberry and poison oak were just getting their new, lime-green leaves. Only an occasional car passed on the old highway bridge nearby. Sitting by the pool with my notebook, I waited as still as a heron.

Up above, high clouds swam in a pale blue sky. Their reflections brightened the water, hypnotizing me with their slow shimmer. After some time I got the sense someone was watching me, and I looked up to see Brad at the top of the bank, the sun glowing behind his cap.

"I saw your car," he said.

It'd been months since I'd thought of him in botanical terms, but I still couldn't meet his eyes as he climbed down the bank. He sat not ten feet away, and I kept my gaze on the water. He knew to be quiet as we kept watch for the fish. After a while of sitting by the stream, hearing it sieve through the shallows, we warmed to a bit of conversation. Brad said he'd been back in Alaska, his home base. He'd grown up fishing for salmon, then had followed various jobs until he ended up here. "It was good to be home," he said. "Though it was colder than a polar bear's ass. But the fish there! Still as big as baby dolphins." He showed me their size with his hands. "Not many steelhead, though."

As if called up, two steelhead edged into the pool right before us. Not the size of Brad's Alaskan salmon, but still more than a foot-and-a-half, tip to tail. First they were just a ripple, then rising sleek bodies. Then they were a couple dancing like foam in an eddy.

"It's a pair!" he said. "Two adults."

Moving together, they slid up the rumpled water of the

riffle. In the flow from a higher pool, they stopped and hovered like hawks. Brad and I got a good look. The doe, a few inches shorter than the buck, lay low while he drifted above her. He guarded her left, then quivered back to her right, more than once blowing back in the current. When that happened he had to push back stronger to regain his place at her side.

Just as I wondered where the combative young trout were, two six-inch male rainbows darted in from upstream.

Brad pointed. "There are the jacks!"

They greased in past the buck like sports cars slipping by a long-haul semi. Working into place beside the doe, they stayed for only three seconds before the buck fought them off. When the current separated him and his intended, he gathered his wits and struggled back to her. Over and over, the jacks darted in; over and over the buck pushed in and edged them out.

"It's got to be his milt," Brad said. "Or nobody's."

The drama played on for the next ten minutes. The doe held her place as the buck acted as sentry to her carnal treasure. All of this happened in three square feet of streambed—one little patch of gravel and cobble and life-giving fluid. Life and death, DNA and evolution, all right there on the ground. I couldn't breathe for the passion of the courtship before us.

Just as I thought the jacks might whip the buck, they gave up and drifted away. "Now it's time," I said.

In a sudden move like the dead zinging back to life, the female rolled over, her body a long blade sweeping the current. She used water as a tool to shift a handful of gravel in the creek.

"She's digging in!" Brad raised himself from his haunches. Without thinking, he cast a shadow over the pool.

The doe and buck steelhead ruffled the water as they fled downstream.

"No!" Brad held his head in his hands.

"'No' is right," boomed a voice. "Shouldn't scare them like that, son." Brad and I both startled. Across the creek stood Harry Cabot-Boon, a big-bodied vintner who grew grapes on land over there. He rested his big hands on his massive hips. His Red Wing boots and blue jeans worn with a nice dress shirt signaled loud and clear that he worked in both the field and office. "Sorry," he said. "Didn't mean to frighten you." He grinned.

Bending to my pen and notebook, I wished I could disappear. Cabot-Boon was never pleasant out on the creek. In town he wasn't bad; but outdoors, he got downright rude. As if he owned the whole valley and we who did not violated some code. Brad made conversation with him, though, friendly and joking across the water. While they spoke I made notes about the spawning ritual we'd just witnessed.

Brad asked, "Hey, Harry, R.J. says the creek's been going dry here. Seen anybody drawing water out of these pools?"

Cabot-Boon looked at his watch. "Sorry. Love to chat but got to run. Let's pick this up again soon."

After Cabot-Boon left with the same stealth as before, the fish returned. The female resumed her dance while the male held there, looking like he'd wait all his life for completion. Once the doe finished making her nest and squeezed out her eggs in a soft mass, the buck released his pent-up stream in a milky cloud. His face was turned away from me, but I knew how he'd look: mouth slack, body trembling, eyes wide open in a silent shriek.

As the male let loose, Brad leaned into me. He circled my waist with his arms, pressing his mouth to the back of my neck. His lips felt like a blaze on my skin. I didn't fight him, but I checked to make sure Cabot-Boon was really gone. To my relief there was nothing over there but trees and blackberry. I let my weight relax against Brad, free falling.

After that Brad and I went out into the watershed every week. We saw everything—adult steelhead in the pools on Radigan Creek, squawfish lurking like piranha below Parson Dam, mitten crabs scuttling on the old bridge piers at Agua Fria Road. We shared long lunches beside pretty pools at the Esperanza-Fox confluence and detoured a few times to the waterfall where nursery fish would gather in summer. I showed him the sucking hoses and the deaths by drying. He said there was nothing we could do. I argued that we had to do something.

Then, on a day in April with only a hint of heat, we circled back to the spawning site near the old highway bridge. We saw the fry, brand new, thick as ants on a mound. They were steelies, not even two inches long. Brad scooped one up with his hands, the little thing tender and see-through on the lifeline of his palm. The baby fish gasped as water ran out between Brad's fingers.

My heart thumped hard. "Put it back!"

He lowered his hand to the stream, murmuring. The steelie floated rigid in the shallow water above his skin. Brad looked stunned. "But it was just a few seconds."

"Those tiny things can't make it for long out here." My breath came out jagged. I opened my notebook and clicked open my pen to record the death.

"You can't write about it!" His eyes were wide. "I just broke the law. Hell, even if it'd lived it could be considered a take."

"A take."

"You know! A capture. Under the Endangered Species Act."

"Of course I know. It's jargon for *murder*."

He swept the steelie out to the sand. Then he walked to his truck without saying goodbye.

The little fish lay at my feet. Already sunken, it was becoming part of the sandy earth. I could wait and make a note of its fate—whether a heron got it for lunch or a raccoon discovered it. Or whether it would just keep drying out and turn to dust. The sight of it hurt me under my sternum. I gathered my gear and headed for my car.

Brad stayed away again and, in a fit of loneliness, I consented to dinner out with the local poet. We spent one long, dull evening where he regaled me with quotations. "So romantic," he said, "that you're playing hard to get. 'To wait Eternity—is short—If Love's reward the end'—Emily Dickinson." He lifted his glass of chardonnay. As he dropped me home, he said, "'The course of true love never did run smooth'—Shakespeare, *A Midsummer Night's Dream*." He called me later to say what a fine time he'd had, and I let the machine take it. Later I dialed Lahaina but hung up before the connection clicked through.

The days brought more sun, more drying. Spring left in a hurry—a few wet storms passed, and summer followed with no warning. The pools were dropping, the fish crowding like refugees into what water remained. They had grown a few inches longer and stronger in their bodies, like seedlings that get to be trees. They needed space; they needed water. At the spawning site near the old highway bridge, a mass of them had gathered in a four-inch-deep pool. At the rate things were going, they'd be stranded in a week.

The sun bore down. Cars hummed by at intervals. A black phoebe flitted between the creek and a cottonwood, going after insects. I studied the pool and listened to traffic noise until, numb and unable to think straight, I left. A mile down the road, I realized I'd forgotten my notebook and had to go back. Returning to park in my usual spot, I slipped toward the creekbank where the phoebe was still trying for bugs. That's when I saw it: a wet ring. The water had dropped two inches. A crown of damp soil rimmed the top of the pool, which had been higher not ten minutes before. The fish were crammed into the remaining water, no flow going in or out. They looked like a mass of worms, writhing, struggling to get wet enough to breathe.

Someone had to be pumping water from the creek. In the dry season, in the middle of the day. Maybe they had rights, and maybe they'd been grandfathered in before the new rules, but they were killing the commons. What to do? I couldn't get my net and bucket and evacuate the fish—moving endangered species was a crime. Brad had been clear that I could be accused of a take. I'd read up on it in the days since: one farmer in the south valley was facing jail time for transferring rare red-legged frogs from one pond to another on his own property. He'd already paid ten grand in fines.

I ran upstream, hopping rocks. Most of the creekbed was dry, but remnant pools held mud that sucked at my shoes each time I landed. Blackberry vines snagged and ripped my shirt as I pushed past. Willow limbs whipped my skin, leaving catkin bits on my arms. A low-hanging branch knocked off my hat, but I didn't stop for it. I kept on toward the machine noise and gurgle of air and water I was seeking. In a moment I almost tripped on a length of black hose. Three inches in diameter and dozens of feet long, it meandered snake like from the creekbed, up the bank and into the brush. I yanked on the hose but couldn't budge it. I tried to rip it open, but it was too strong. At last I picked up a piece of dark glassy rock with sharp edges—obsidian, I guess—and attacked it. I pounded, pounded, and gashed until I made a big hole. Then I continued hacking until I tore off three feet to take as evidence. The pump rumbled and inhaled air.

Hose in hand, I ran to my car and started driving. I had no plan. I had to force myself to pause at the stop signs. If the pools could drop two inches in ten minutes, what would be left by the end of the day? Not enough water to cover a single pair of gills. Maybe there'd be suffocation by the dozens. By the hundreds.

I found myself heading for the government offices at city hall. When I parked and hurried inside, I didn't see Brad's truck five spaces away. I burst through the front door to the offices, hose in hand, realizing too late I'd pushed in on some kind of meeting. The people sat in chairs facing the front of the room, and they turned to look at me. There were dairy farmers, vintners, men from the local water board—all well groomed and pressed in business clothes. Harry Cabot-Boon was there, stuffed into the same grower costume as always, surrounded by a group of buddies. There was the president of the golf club, the superintendent of parks and recreation, a few of the city maintenance guys. The mayor. Only one other woman was in sight, typing up minutes in the front of the room.

Brad stood behind the podium, frozen midsentence. "Hello, R.J.," he said, his first words to me in weeks. "Have a seat."

"I can't. The fish are out of water!"

I knew my pants were hemmed in mud, my shirt snagged by blackberry thorns. No doubt my face had tear streaks down it and my hair hung in a tangle.

There were murmurs all around.

Brad put up his hands to quiet the crowd. "Yes," he said, so all could hear. "That's why we're meeting. To work on an MOU for Aquatic Species."

I stared at him, not comprehending.

"A Memorandum of Understanding," he explained. "It'll be signed and active in six months."

"Six months!" I held up the section of black hose, the proof of water thievery he'd been seeking. "I found this in the creek. Just now. Pumping it dry."

Brad kept his expression neutral. He held papers in a sheaf

above the podium.

"Brad. They'll die if we don't move them."

"They may die if we do." Droplets of sweat rimmed his eyebrows.

A voice boomed from the audience. "You know," said Cabot-Boon. "Moving those endangered fish is against the law." The crowd murmured its agreement. Someone chuckled.

"Right." Brad nodded. "It'd be a take."

I turned to the plump, well-watered bodies squeezed into chairs. My cheeks were flushed, I knew. Forcing myself to meet their eyes, I held up the length of hose. "Isn't this a take, too?" I turned to Brad. "Isn't it? Taking water that kills the fish?"

"This yours?" I faced Cabot-Boon. "Or yours?" I asked another grower I'd seen in the papers, a millionaire wine heir barely out of college. His sat with his mouth hanging open, like he'd never signed up for such a life, and shifted his gaze to the floor. All the growers did, one by one. No one owned the hoses. The room grew as hushed as the city morgue.

In a moment Brad took my arm as if I were sick or injured and guided me toward the door. I pulled away. He latched onto me again, harder this time, so I let him lead me down the aisle. There was silence around us, until we reached the last row. Then someone behind us hissed, "Fish lady."

I whipped around. They all kept their eyes away. No one seemed to have spoken.

Brad walked me outside to my car. "Don't mess things up, R.J. I'm serious." He abandoned me there—hose in my hand. He left me alone, dirty, and afraid, and he returned to the meeting with the men in chairs.

That night the moon waxed full, and I had the classical hour on again. This time I lay in bed on top of my sheets, eyes open, feeling the weight of the heat. Even with the windows open, my bedroom was as stuffy as a schoolhouse. The sweats hadn't yet hit, and I prayed they wouldn't. My radio played Brahms, whose name always makes me think of lullabies, but this was a rowdy piece: the "Academic Festival Overture." All the strings buzzed away, so busy, working toward a peak. As I lay there listening to the action, I felt nowhere near slumber. The humming of the strings sounded more like insects than music.

I thought of cicadas, then the willows they inhabit, then the creek they border. My mind went to the fish again. Canaries in the coal mine. If they dried up and spirited away, we wouldn't be far behind. We lived in the same web of water, the same strand of survival. As I pondered it, a call came in to my answering machine. "R.J., it's Bob. Great news! I've met someone in Lahaina, she's really special. Please pick up, I know you're there . . . " I tuned him out. The entire orchestra was still building.

In a rush, after taking forever to get there, the piece reached a climax that lasted just sixty seconds. Sixty seconds! The moment came and went that fast. As the music swelled, I felt my body rise with it, something inside me that surfaced like a trout to a fly.

Enough. I got up, pulled on my clothes, and slipped out of the house. Heading for my car, I picked up gear from my shed: dip net, bucket, water shoes, headlamp. The moon had climbed high overhead. I could have driven with my headlights off, it was so bright. But I didn't. I kept on as normally as possible to the old highway bridge and the spawning site. Not wanting to be seen from any of the country homes, I continued past my usual pull-off. I didn't even turn my head to look and didn't slow down until I'd made it around the corner and into an ash grove. Then, switching off my lights, I left my car well hidden. There was no traffic. No one would see me walk to the bridge

184

and climb down to the pool.

By the light of the moon, I could tell the water had risen again. At the water's edge, I switched on my headlamp. In the glow I could see steelies who hadn't made it: a half dozen floated belly-up on the water's surface. Others lay dead at the edge of the pool. I picked one up—it was wrinkled, like it'd been freeze-dried, its eyeballs crumpled in a lifeless stare. My own eyes blurred with tears. My heart bounded like something made of rubber in my chest.

I scooped dead steelies out of the water. Then I dipped the net back in for live ones. After several tries—close calls, I was still getting the knack—I heard someone coming, creeping down the road in a vehicle. Clicking off my headlamp, I drew my gear under the bridge. A truck passed above me and parked. Headlights switched off. A boot crunched on gravel.

I listened and waited. My heart still pumped like a machine you can't turn off. A flashlight beam played on the creek bank, then the gravel bar, then the water. I glanced at the pool and . . . my bucket! White as a July moon, it was still sitting at the rim of the pool near the dead steelies. I withdrew farther into the shadow under the bridge.

A flashlight beam traveled from the truck to the pool. It continued to the bucket, passed it, then returned to the bucket and snapped off. There was the sound of footsteps, the sight of boots, a pair of jeans, and a torso in a light jacket. A shaved head shone in the moonlight. Brad, out of uniform. He picked up the bucket and peered around. He stood a minute, looking and listening.

He switched his flashlight back on, studying the pool, his face reflected in the glow off the water. Many moments passed, as if he were counting, thinking. Then he held the flashlight in his teeth and bent close to the water. He dipped in with the bucket, lighting his way with the wandering beam. I saw him try and miss, again and again, and heard him curse. They were getting away from him.

I moved out of hiding and switched on my headlamp. "That won't work."

Brad dropped the bucket.

"You're going to need this instead." I extended my dip net to him.

He let out his breath. "I'm sorry, R.J." He came to me and touched my cheek. "I've been a total dick."

I felt the crazy beating settle down in my heart. "And I've been a . . . fish lady."

"Come on," he said. "We can move them to a better pool upstream."

I nodded, and we got busy. We found we didn't need our lights, the moon was bright enough. We caught steelie after steelie, more than you might've thought were there just by looking. It was a cinch—Brad used the dip net as I held a bucket of water, and we transferred the little fish upstream to a deep pool under a full canopy of oak and bay. As we worked together, we made sure no steelie was out of the water for more than a few seconds. Longer than that, we both knew, would be too long.

No Way Bay

George Victor sensed he would die young; the darkness was in his blood. His mother and two sisters watched him with vigilance, as eagles watch the river. The plea never left the women's eyes, the prayer that he not follow the path taken by his father and brothers. Not even his mother came straight out and begged, though she could have, he knew. Her hope for his long life emanated in unspoken words, and her wishes for his safety hovered always. He answered her concerns with, "I'm careful in the skiff—I don't drink, I follow the rules, I know the tides." She and his sisters relaxed at this reassurance, but George knew their fear lingered. In his family, despair had a history of overriding caution and trumping hope.

George Sr. had described their bad luck as a dark vision. "I think things will turn around, and then I see blackness, like the deepest part of the ocean." Two days later, he vanished from the family troller, the *Ocean Eagle*, when a windstorm blew up the inlet and battered the boat as he tried to secure its mooring. His remains washed to shore near the ferry loading ramp, where they were spotted by a tourist. George's mother and sister wailed for days, while George maintained a silent bafflement over his father's inability to save himself so close to land. One year and a day later, George's three older brothers died at sea: Henry, John, and Roy all lost together in a squall that blew up out of a calm morning. The *Ocean Eagle* went down with them. George had been too sick to fish that day. Bad clam chowder from the Shiner Diner had emptied him out. He woke the next morning to learn he'd lost half his remaining family overnight and, in the many months since, he hadn't crewed on any boat besides his red skiff.

He wore the Victor family traits in the way one wears skin: thick dark hair, sturdy build, sharp eyes that missed nothing. The apartment where he lived near his mother and sisters was as bright as possible for a coastal hometown that got ninety inches of rainfall a year and forty inches of snow. On his dark days, a feeling settled on George blacker than a raven's eyes after sundown—an inky hopelessness that matched his father's vision of the bottomless sea. But when his inherited gloom or the weather didn't oppress him, breezes through the spruce and alder on shore carried hope. On his light days, he knew the salmon spawning, dying, and stinking up the rivers outside of town meant not just inevitable loss. It also meant the fish were still out there if he could just get to them.

George was a good troller. He took pride in hooking and cleaning chinook, coho, and chum salmon and treating each one with respect. He knew how to keep the fish fresh and unbruised before shipping. Trolling topped his list of things worth doing, but it was impossible without the *Eagle*. He and his brothers had struggled enough with the complex maze of licenses, season start and end dates, fishing limits, and area closures. The sinking of the troller had sounded the death knell for the family business. Life had been much better when tribal tradition was the overarching law keeping balance in their world. Back then, according to George Sr., his family had earned more than enough from fishing to live on, sell at market, and share at potlatch. The restrictions that came later pushed them to the edge. They hadn't been carrying insurance on the *Eagle* for two years, leaving George stranded when it sunk.

He did have a job, sort of. One day he'd agreed to motor the Fish and Game warden around the inlet, and it had turned into a regular paying gig. George used his skiff, which still had its original red paint and the fifteen-horsepower Suzuki motor his father had bought to replace an ancient but powerful Merc. Though sturdy, the skiff was plagued by leaking floor seams, and George couldn't keep ahead of their continual loosening. He sealed them as often as he could stand to bring the boat out of the water, put it under tarps, and dry it to the extent the southeast Alaska weather allowed. Even flawed, the skiff came to be one piece of his world George could trust.

He suspected the warden, Brad, was capable of exploring the inlet on his own. Brad had access to all kinds of boats at his job, and he was a smart guy with lots of friends. He'd grown up in Alaska, come back after fishing down south, and knew his way around motors and oars. His wife, R.J., was some sort of boater and steelhead expert now studying salmon, and she came in the skiff, too. Those two seemed to prefer that George guide them—that was obvious. They asked discreet questions, but they couldn't hide their fascination with native wisdom. What ancient fishing customs did you learn from your tribe? How did your elders explain the way salmon find their way home?

George returned polite but brief answers. He didn't want to lose the job, but talking about the tribe turned a good day bad in a hurry. It was tough enough to have to make a living touring around with a couple from down south without being reminded of the old, lost ways. He'd rather motor solo any day and forget the talk. Even when his father and brothers were alive, George would sometimes go alone in the skiff on his days off. He'd steal away to throw out single lines in No Way Bay and keep only solitude for company. That bay attracted few boaters, divided as it was from the inlet by a channel that filled with boat-eating whitewater when the tide hurried back out to sea.

Whenever George motored near the boat harbor, he'd check to see if Calvin had opened his workshop doors. If so, George aimed for shore, docked the skiff, and walked the long block to visit the master carver. George would sit on a tree-stump seat while Calvin labored over cedar poles, his long, silver-streaked hair held back in a ponytail. Calvin was from farther southeast but had come to town at least a decade before. He'd converted a garage on the main street into a workshop open to the sidewalk, where he kept bistro stools and a coffee cart. Tools hung on a red-and-black pegboard behind him. When cruise ships arrived, or even the state ferries, he put out a sandwich sign inviting passersby to watch him cut and repaint wood.

Now Calvin was rehabilitating a totem that had been cracking, as poles did over time. He'd removed the bolts and nails used in earlier attempts to hold the wood together. "Allowing it to split helps relieve pressure in the cedar. It's what the tree wants to do."

Calvin couldn't always give George his full attention, as the visitors' questions often absorbed him. Then George sat listening, smoking hand-rolled tobacco. He enjoyed the carver's storytelling and full, deep voice. Today Calvin spoke to a handful of tourists who'd been shuttled from the latest cruise ship that was moored, as many-windowed and imposing as a small city, just offshore.

"This is the Russian lord." Calvin pointed to the squat human figure at the top of the pole. "Farther down here we have the chief from the Raven clan." Other emblems—Bear, Frog, and Eagle—sat above and below the chief, although none dwarfed him. All were receiving new paint. Now Calvin was refreshing the whiteness of Eagle's head.

"How'd the Russian get to be top guy on the totem pole?" asked a big man wearing a *Red Sox* ballcap. His poncho, one of the white PVC handouts sprinkled with tiny blue *Alaska!* logos, hung just past his crotch.

A woman with frizzed red hair whispered, "Peter, don't."

Calvin smiled. "Joining different cultures in the art form represents well-being among nations. It's a peace pole."

"Well said!" remarked Peter, a bit too loud to George's ears.

George wanted to add, "Yeah, and the dude farther down the pole is the baddest-ass," but he stayed silent.

After the visitors left, George rose from the stump-seat to view the progress on Frog. He waited before asking, "How can you say that shit about peace between nations?"

Calvin straightened up, reaching his full height. He was a head taller than George, and now his eyes were wide. "Even my Grandfather Jacob wouldn't call it shit."

"My grandfathers are dead."

Calvin set aside his paintbrush. "Mine, too. But they showed me how to go on. Especially Grandfather Jacob. I mean, here was a man . . . his only son—my father—was killed trying to break up a bar fight in Juneau. His wife—my grandmother—died of tuberculosis at forty. He lost his will to carve, too, after a bad deal with a trader." Calvin shook his head. "Grandfather's last piece, a Killer Whale bowl, took him a year to make, starting with the cutting of the wood. He held all the ceremonies, everything done the old way. After the trader took his money and never made good on the sale, he reported it to the borough. But no one could help him, or so they said. He never did another piece."

Calvin shook his head and went back to painting. "I thought I could live in both worlds—here and on Taan, or so-called Prince of Wales Island. But I don't go there now. Most of the villages have been raided. Stuff was carried off, even the burial boxes." Calvin looked up. His face and voice revealed no bitterness.

"My mother lives in Ketchikan. You know that, I visit her sometimes. She stays away from Taan, too. Fortunately Grandfather Jacob taught me to carve to help keep that old world alive."

George stared at his feet, wishing he were back in the skiff. If other visitors came, he'd slip out before there was more talk. No one else wandered in, though, and he stayed at the shop until the mouth of the inlet glowed with midday sun.

"You going home for lunch, George? Or should I ask Freda to add a plate to our table?"

George stood to leave. He wanted to head up to No Way Bay while light still brightened the opposite shore. "No thanks, Calvin. I'm going back to the skiff."

Gloom overtook George as he motored from the dock. Wind had come up on the inlet. He hadn't checked the tide book, but he knew the falling sea would soon be sieving through the rocks in the channel to the bay. It became most dangerous at ebb tide. He'd been out there before in dicey conditions—jockeying the skiff in the current like buck salmon fighting jacks, ignoring the warnings about the ice-cold bay and the prior accidents there. It wasn't intentional, he realized; it was just that the slate-gray rocks and flashing rapids drew him. He thought of his mother's pleading eyes and waved them off with a swipe of his hand.

As he drove up the inlet, his darkness deepened. He brooded on everything lost and the things he couldn't do. Or have. Thousands of people stepped off the ships every day with more money than God. They paraded through town in designer hiking boots, carrying sacks of goods from the boutiques. He was well aware how many valuable dollars that could buy a new troller were being thrown at stuffed puffins and imitation fur-trader hats.

Twenty grand. That was what he needed. He laughed and heard his own anger. Might as well wish for a mansion in Cedar Heights.

He gripped the gunnel of the red skiff with his free hand. Autumn filled the air. So did the burnt-tire stench of pink salmon spawning and dying in Russian Creek. Light angled into the spruce-green slopes ringing the inlet. Water splashed in the bottom of his boat where a few rivets were leaking again. He felt his fury rise and then remembered Calvin. He wished he had the carver's calm. He should have accepted the offer for lunch.

The tide had turned. Only a wet ring remained on shore below the sharp tree boundary. Good. By the time he motored into the channel, conditions might be perfect for running the rapids. Out of habit he checked the straps on his lifejacket, chafed at its confinement, and unfastened it. He let it fall to the bottom of the boat. Lifejackets hadn't saved his father or his brothers.

To his left, a humpback whale surfaced and shot mist twenty feet in the air.

"Christ!" George about fell off his seat. He settled again, heart pounding, as the whale rolled down. Another one, much smaller, surfaced, too—once, twice, three times—forcing out a cloud and rush of air on each emergence. On the fourth rising, the small whale raised itself higher, showing more dorsal fin, then plunged deeper, displaying its young flukes as if they were new wings. The mother rose again, blowing a thunderous plume of salt water and waving her own shimmering, mature flukes before disappearing. George smiled, observed himself smiling, and scowled. He'd always heard you're not close to a whale unless you smell its primal, oceanic breath, but he could smell nothing. Even they were distant from him on this day. "It doesn't matter," he muttered.

Reaching the rocky channel that led to the bay, George could see in a moment that the tide wasn't as low as he'd hoped. He cursed the ocean—and immediately regretted it. "It's my own fault," he admitted. "For not checking ahead." He called to the ocean, asking forgiveness. He was still subject to the beliefs of his people, he knew. His father had taught him that those who respected nature lived and died by it. Those who did not were on their own, neither aided nor fazed by their ignorance. A flatliner's life, in George's opinion.

A silver cabin cruiser entered the channel from the far end. It was a government rig, George guessed, although he couldn't yet make out an insignia. Radar rotated on a pole near the steering well. The cruiser rumbled toward him, then throttled down and drew within thirty feet of his skiff. It was Fish and Game. The captain cut the engine and called to him through a megaphone.

"Personal floatation devices are required."

Damn. It was Brad, in raingear, watch cap, and an orange lifejacket. He drifted closer. "Hey, George! Didn't see that was you. Here, let me lend you a PFD."

George smiled but didn't speak. He picked up his own lifejacket, threaded his arms through it, and snapped the buckles. He shrugged and smiled bigger.

"Trying to get yourself killed?" Brad shook his finger in mock scolding. "It's getting bad in the channel. You should see the chop back there. Let's run back to town together."

George almost turned him down. But he remembered there'd be a pole raising the next day, and everybody he knew would be there. Tomorrow he could slip back up to No Way

Bay unnoticed. He shrugged again. "Sure," he said, feeling the blackness press on him with an even greater weight.

It was an Eagle day. Damn. George knew it as soon as he woke to a clear sky and stood at his window scanning the shore. Bald eagles perched on the posts near his skiff. Later in the morning, cormorants would claim those same spots, and by evening gulls would take them over and not budge for hours. But now there were four eagles—two standing motionless on the posts and two more that came and went. None was accomplishing much that George could see. They seemed to be resting, the way a cat does, saving energy for important work later.

Eagles inspired confusion in George. In the stories his father had told him when he was little, Eagle meant power. In those tales Eagle swept down from the mountains like Thunderbird, filled with great purpose. The eagles George observed in real life, however, spent most of their time picking over trash heaps. What did they have in common with the great, fierce Thunderbird?

His mother called on the land line, the only telephone George had since the family cell phone plan expired. "George," she whispered. "Your father and brothers are watching you today."

"What? From where?"

"Shh! Not so loud. You'll scare them off. Haven't you looked outside?"

"Mom, it's just pink salmon season. Eagles are everywhere."

"But four of them? Down by your boat? They know you're up to something."

"Not true. I'm up to almost nothing."

"I'll call Christine and Martha to go out fishing with you."

His sisters. "That won't help."

"Then go see Calvin. He called last night. He wants to know if you're coming to the Peace Pole raising this evening."

"No, Mom, he must've called to invite you. You're the one on the intertribal council."

"The raising's at sundown on the square. Everyone will be there, both tribes, all the clans, all—"

"I'll go see Calvin." George hung up without hearing the rest.

He was aware of his own disrespect, cutting off his mother's speech. But the familiar feeling was descending. If he let it fall farther, he might use stronger words. Worse, it would paralyze him, and he would never get out of his apartment.

He tried to think. A pole raising meant there'd be feasting. The New Potlatch, they called it. New Potlatch meant they'd invite everyone, even those from outside both tribes. The guests would eat and laugh and drink like they belonged there or knew the meaning of the gathering. He looked at his socks, thinking about putting them on his feet. Several minutes passed. He wanted his troller back.

He checked his tide book. Out of habit his eyes went first to the symbol that ranked fishing conditions. It showed a big fish for good fishing today. Damn. In the old days he would've been out there already. His shoes would've been on his feet in seconds. He looked at the time for low tide—it would have to be the afternoon low since he'd missed the morning. Lowest tide at four twenty-one. Good. That was about the time everyone would be getting ready for the pole raising.

He'd told his mother he'd go see Calvin, and he would have, but the carver's doors were closed when George motored past. Just as well. He felt a strong urge to get to No Way Bay even before the tide fell. Maybe he could drive up and cast a line out for salmon without having to see anybody. Brad wouldn't be patrolling the same waters a second day in a row. And there'd be the thrill of rapids in the channel at the end of the day.

George kept his speed slow across the inlet. The sky was still as clear as fresh snowmelt, with a warm wind from the east. Too warm. Maybe it was the warming he'd been warned would come: George Sr. had said the whole world would slip so far out of balance that ice fields would thaw. Polar bears would mate with brown bears. Whales would shift the season and distance of their migrations. "How soon is that coming?" George had asked.

His father didn't know or wouldn't say. "It's something your grandfather told me. Passed down from his father." Grandfather had said that all through the ages warming had wiped out tribes that got too far from their center. But the new warming would be worldwide, as if the Earth itself had heat like the sun and nothing in the universe could cool it.

George often forgot about the warming. On a day like today, though, the breeze reminded him. It felt too hot for a trip to glacier-lined No Way Bay. A melting wind when he was that close to ice unnerved him.

Still he aimed his skiff for the channel. As he neared the opening in the wooded coastline, he felt the confinement of his lifejacket again. He undid the buckles and threw it onto the floor of the skiff, frowning as the orange vest fell in water that had seeped through the rivets. Even as he saw the material dampen and darken, he knew he was foolish. With the shadow growing in him, though, he was powerless to change.

When he reached the bay, the repeated surfacing of pink salmon started him fishing. It wasn't so hot near the thick forest that hemmed the rocky shore. He hadn't brought a cooler, but he did have his knife. He cut cedar boughs that hung close to the water. They'd hold his catch on the aluminum floor where it curved highest and stayed dry, far in the bow. The day passed with ease as he sat with line out. Between the sunlight and the warmth of the breeze, which he forgot to abhor, he lost track of time. He felt lighter as the hours dissolved. Although he had left his license home, he knew his limit. When he reached it, he decided to motor back down the channel, across the inlet, and into town to share his bounty at the pole raising. He hummed, thinking of how his mother and sisters would smile.

The tide had fallen. By the looks of things, it might even be reaching slack. He drifted toward the channel, out of the bay. Black boulders that had been under water now cut the surface— or worse, lurked just beneath. The channel frothed with the speed of the tide racing to sea, gripping the skiff and drawing it toward the emerging rocks. George had been floating without power; now he needed the motor to ferry, and fast. Damn. It took between one and five pulls to start it, and in the way of many mechanical things, it would balk if he panicked.

He pulled the start-cord. Nothing. A second pull. Nothing. A third pull, and the Suzuki coughed to life. With his heart jumping, George aimed back up the channel at full throttle and sped away from the rocks. The engine whined, a buzz-saw sound too full of air for his comfort. Not a good time to cavitate. He checked over his shoulder. Good, he had put distance between himself and the worst of the boulders.

Back up in the bay, uptide from the risky channel, he reassessed. He pulled his lifejacket out of the water on the floor and snapped it on. As he drifted back down, he felt the tidal current grab him again. It was fast. There was no way he could trust the dinky motor to help him thread the rocks. His heart pounded as he tried to think.

The oars. He'd row his way through.

Fitting the eight-foot oars into the locks cost him time, but George got them in place and rowed. Too late. The skiff crunched onto an underwater reef—a coward, his father used to call those sleepers. George felt the boat pivot on the rock mass. He shifted his weight to allow the floor to slip free. It was a bad scrape but hadn't ripped aluminum. Good.

He pulled two full strokes as the boat swept toward a small comb of black boulders at the channel's edge. He cursed as he crabbed a blade that canted the boat. The right gunnel almost scooped water. Leaning left, he lifted the diving oar, and the boat righted.

His breath, full of fear, sounded like a gale to him. He dreaded the water. If he fell out or capsized, the chill would allow him just fifteen minutes before numbing him senseless. That wouldn't be enough time for George: he'd dropped out of swimming lessons before learning anything but dogpaddle. And there'd be no rescue, no warm hold of a boat's cabin. No one would be there to save him. Everyone would be at the town square, laying out guideline ropes for the pole raising.

His imagination worked overtime. He pictured his lungs about to burst as he sunk and held his breath. He could see the first small bubble leaving his lips, followed by an uncontrollable balloon of his last, precious oxygen, as his limbs turned to ice blocks.

He shook off the image. Ahead, the current foamed among the same rocks that had troubled him earlier. Now they appeared as a stony arm a foot above water, reaching halfway across the channel. He'd have to pull hard left to avoid them. He angled the boat to ferry, feeling water speed under the floor, hoping the leaking rivets would hold. The arm of rock, wet and glinting light, drew current and the boat as if in command of its tiller. George needed more floatation. He needed more power.

As occurs in boating crises, time became elastic. What were likely only seconds felt like long minutes that stretched and bent and filled with uncertainty. In those moments, George sensed the icy blackness his father had known. He saw his brothers' faces, now white with long sleep.

From somewhere inside him came the prayer. "Everlasting one! Everlasting one! Put your hand under us." Chanting, he rowed so hard the oars bowed. "Everlasting one! Everlasting one! Raise us up!" George didn't watch his progress, he just prayed and pulled.

He didn't stop rowing until he felt the current slow, and knew he was far enough left. In a moment he floated toward the smooth, open water of the inlet.

Crumpling over the oars, he inhaled. With each breath his fear subsided. A trembling that had gripped him eased. As it did, his wonder increased at the prayer that had come from an unremembered place—a story of his father's? Something his mother had shared? He didn't know. "Thank you!" he called to the sky. Above him an eagle winged north toward town. At the top of his lungs, George called to it. "Thank you!"

He lifted his oars from the locks and set them back inside the boat. He moved to the rear of the skiff. With a single, purposeful tug, he started the motor.

He aimed for town, where lights would be coming on in the square. Soon the elders would invite everyone to help lift the pole, and folks he knew would be rushing out of the darkness to help. He would see his mother there, and Calvin. The carver might not notice him driving back across the inlet, but he'd be sure to see George join the crowd on the ropes. His sisters would nod their approval in the warm breeze of the evening. Maybe their eyes would be clear of their usual plea to him. They'd remark on what a fine string of pinks George had brought for potlatch. The warden Brad would be there, too, with R.J., but he wouldn't ask to check any license. He'd probably just join George and his family at their table as they all sat down for the feast.

ACKNOWLEDGMENTS

My deepest respect and most sincere admiration go to my maternal grandfather, Austin Frost of Nunda, New York, for his manuscript, "Accelerating Theory of Earth Development: An Exposition" (1977). His life as a naturalist, boatman, and amateur scientist inspired the story, "An Exposition of the Development of the Earth." Although we never achieved our dream of being coauthors, Austin's curiosity and passion for the outdoors thrive in my pen every day. My maternal grandmother, Marjorie Conrad Frost, handed down a legacy of music, creativity, acceptance, and support for the work of others that lives on in my heart.

My paternal grandfather, Russell Lawton, Sr., of Fall River, Massachusetts, died when I was very young. My parents' memories of him, as well as faded family photographs and movies on 8 mm film, confirm his gentle nature. He always wanted to see his four grandchildren grown and to learn what we'd do with our lives. Instead, a blood disease possibly related to his work as a machinist claimed him before any of us grew out of grade school. My paternal grandmother, Jenny Cook Lawton, was an independent spirit and accomplished painter.

Her artist's eye saw all.

These four loving individuals raised my awareness of the importance of nature, clean water, artistic expression, and, most of all, family. My stories would not be what they are without my grandparents' various gifts to me.

Deepest gratitude to Lillian Howan, Jill Koenigsdorf, Karen Laws, and Z Egloff, who reviewed these stories in early drafts and made helpful suggestions. Many thanks as well to Russ and Marge Lawton and my siblings, Tim, Jen, and Jon, for reading and commenting on my treatment of places they know and love. Thanks to Kat Wilder, a true friend, sensitive writer, and supporter through everything. To my friends and family who made this book possible with your monetary contributions toward publication, I'm forever in your debt. And, always, much affection and many thanks to my husband, Paul Christopulos, and my daughter, Rose McMackin, who shared this literary journey step by step. I would never survive a world without you all in it.

And my appreciation to Roger Real Drouin and all the staff at Little Curlew Press for adopting and publishing this collection—for the good of wild places and free-flowing rivers. May Little Curlew Press's faith in these words and my writer's life truly float all boats.

This book was sponsored in part by Kathryn B. Wilder.